THE INHIBITIONIST

BY

MARC RUSSELL

ALL RIGHTS RESERVED

Publisher's Note:

This is a work of fiction. All names, characters, places, and events are the work of the author's imagination.

Any resemblance to real persons, places, or events is coincidental.

Solstice Publishing - www.solsticepublishing.com

The Inhibitionist

By

Marc Russell

For Lucia, of course.

Preliminaries

Timor Mortis Nobis Dolorem

How many ways does life pass you by?
As days and weeks merge and then the years fly –
What sly intimation of time running out
Reflects in your quantum of fear or of doubt?

Beguiled by distractions, you soon realize
The baubles are hollow, helpless to disguise
The flicker and falter of eyes soon bereft
Of hope, then intention, then most of what's left.

Salve timor mortis, and now that you're here –
Gargantuan, appalling, egregiously clear –
Your glimpse of the nightshade, the curtain, the veil
Says all that we cherish will finally fail.

Our thoughts lose precision, our limbs lose their verve;
Then I'll lose my marbles and you'll lose your nerve.
Not even the energy to count up the ways…

When at the end, we number our days.

Chapter One

Marc

You feel your mortality in your teeth. Not in your flesh, nor your bones: it's your teeth where the trouble starts.

Oh, I'm serious: bear with me.

You lose your milk teeth when you're around six. Some describe them as *deciduous*—implying temporary things that are shed, like blossom or leaves. But you remember the coins under your pillow, don't you? You remember the tooth fairy? Of course you do. You see?

Teeth. Already you were old enough to notice them.

And then—magically—the tooth fairy puts them back in again. You start to take your teeth for granted, right then.

You were also young enough to forget.

After that, barring disasters, poor diet or significant drug abuse, they'll stick around for a while, your teeth. Biting, chewing, helping your smile along, maybe clicking out a rhythm to the tune in your head. They'll almost certainly contribute to the formation of the dental consonant—part of your deployment of that useful human proclivity called language. If you develop a lisp (a misapplication of the dental consonant) you might come in for some ridicule. Blame it on your tongue, not your teeth. Perhaps though, subsequently, they'll be bared: that ancient simian posture from back when teeth were weapons.

Now they're just a part of our rituals of rage and hostility.

You won't much notice them doing any of those things, however. Mostly, they'll just sit there, functional props framed by motile flesh and muscle—passive chips of enamel set in the grooves of your jaws. Part of the furniture in your head.

But later, when you start dying, your teeth will know it first.

Some folks make a case for your hair being fate's barometer. The loss of it, obviously; and yes, it might be a contender for one of the principal signatures of decline. But... it's equivocal. Once you get past the obvious—that hair loss is mainly a man thing—actually, men tend to begin losing their hair in their thirties or forties which is also generally regarded as their prime. So that confounds things before you get started. But then some guys, they lose it in their twenties, which is terrible luck and further erodes the association.

I mean, twentysomethings. They're barely adults these days.

Add to that the facts that baldness is often associated with brilliance and that half the male population have shaved their heads anyway and the correlation is hopelessly bereft.

The same goes for your eyes. They too deteriorate—but the process usually starts simply as a result of growing, and nearly sixty-five percent of the population are wearing specs by early middle age. They're fashion accessories for goodness' sake. So that doesn't really work either.

No. It's your teeth you have to look out for, though we often don't.

They're easily fixed, at first. Shovel in the amalgam. Apply the porcelain. Gargle and swish. Modern dentistry can keep them apparently strong and seemingly gleaming for years. But that soft pulpy nerve at their root is the sweetest treat for the billion bacteria—every one of them looking for their main chance—that call your mouth their home.

And so it starts: the increasing sensitivity, the dull ache, the looseness, the outright agony. Unbearable and unceasing. Then they fall out.

And this time they're not coming back.

Time passes. You can rationalize the first such loss, maybe even the second. But each new absence represents a three percent decline in this now finite roster. You can measure their deterioration in terms that, if it was money we were talking about—I mean if it was money we were talking about *losing*—some people would be thinking of skydiving from their high places.

So there you have it: my thesis on the prime sign of decline in the modern age. You can split hairs. The eyes don't have it. But you can count on teeth.

Teeth are quantitative.

Did you see what I did there? While I sketched out these grim metrics?

I'll tell you:

I gave these signs a sense of place. Of position. The variables I chose to calibrate decrepitude are all rooted in your head. And while that's convenient for my exposition so far it serves a further purpose. It paves the way for the next step, the last lap, the quantum leap. They share another characteristic, these signals of dysfunction: you see, they're all… I was going to say "just physical" but that doesn't quite nail it.

"Corporeal" comes closer. A good word relating to a person's body as opposed to their spirit. Quite apt. And you don't have to prefix it with "just". I'd almost stick with corporeal but for the fact that its distinction between body and spirit is lopsided. The thing I've got to talk about is the spirit as mediated by flesh.

In fact, I don't think I have a word, even though I usually have so many.

So let's put it another way: you can be bald as a badger, blind as a bat, and toothless as a crone, yet still claim your fundamental integrity. You—your "self"—remain intact. Coherent, cohesive and functional. Whereas the thing I've got to talk about, the other thing that's rooted in your head, the most appalling and chronic calibration of decline—the thing I've been avoiding, actually—it robs you of all that.

So here we go.

The two most significant physical manifestations are an excess of neuritic plaques and neurofibrillary tangles. Neuritic plaques are extracellular deposits of beta-amyloid protein in the grey matter of the brain. The beta-amyloid occupies the center of these plaques. Surrounding the protein are fragments of deteriorating neurons, especially those that produce acetylcholine, a neurotransmitter essential for processing memory and learning.

Neurofibrillary tangles are twisted remnants of a protein called tau, which is found inside brain cells and is essential for maintaining proper cell structure and function. An abnormality in the tau protein disrupts normal cell activity.

Amyloid plaques. Deteriorating neurons. Twisted protein remnants. They make losing your hair, sight, or teeth look like a walk in the park.

Teeth, in particular, turned out to be a case of misdirection. A red herring.

Welcome, instead, to Alzheimer's.

Chapter Two

The Inhibitionist

sHeS here agane, the
the she girl. Wuman.
She stokes my hare mi
fase nice. kind
She smel swete like a
flowr. Her got bright
paterns on her arms and
back. Shert all lite an
sparkle
Lu Lu. Lusha. Lucia.
She name is Her name is
Lucia. Lucia. My wife.
She shines like a flame
in my gray worled
Hard to tink. Brief
think only. Gos awaye
so quick

Tea. Gives me tea. Gud.
Worm.
No. Good. Warm. My warm
tea wife gives me warm
tea. Takes cold tea
awaye put down thing
thing caled flush no
cup no sink. Cold tea
down sink.
Such hard werk. Try
more tamoro

Chapter Three

Marc

So. That's me. Pretty messed up, don't you think?

I write those things and then look back at them, trying to forge a link between my fractured states of mind. One thing rings out like a bell: my undivided love for Lucia, my wife. We'll hear from her soon. You'll like her, I'm certain. In the meantime, I'm reading over my words; "She smel swete like a flowr"; "shert all lite an sparkle"; "she shines like a flame in my gray worled"; and "my warm tea wife." To me, knowing her, they have a naïve poetry that describes both her gravity and lightness of being. She's the axis of my existence, my beacon when I'm on the other side. I would be nothing without her.

All that and more.

I've got dementia, you see. Middle stage Alzheimer's disease to be precise. Yes, I know, there's a lot to explain. We'll come to that. But right now, I want to illustrate how, in that "gray worled", *the heart remembers.* Though the parts of the brain that govern emotions and feelings are often among the first to go—they're called the amygdala and hippocampus, parts of the limbic system (just so you know)—despite that, the deepest and strongest neural links are normally the last to depart.

I've loved Lucia deeply and strongly for years. She's a black woman, from Caribbean stock, born a Cockney in the East End of London. We're neither of us old, and she's a little younger than I am. Where nature has been cruel to me, it has been kind to her. While I'm drifting away in different directions, she's neat and firm. Tightly contained within herself. Her light brown skin glows with life and energy. Her dark brown eyes—sometimes almost ebony—are clear and bright. She has an oval face with neatly arranged features that declare her wit and intelligence. Though her nose is slim and straight, she has African lips: thick, rich and ripe with a pronounced philtrum that tugs her upper lip into the shape of a cupid's bow. When she smiles, her teeth are uneven, the result of a playground accident that was never fixed properly. She hates her teeth, but I adore them. They're survivors. She has a long body, full, high breasts and strong athletic arms and legs. Her hands and feet are delicate, slender things. Her buttocks are firm and round. A black woman's arse.

There's not a part of her I haven't revered, nor worshipped, nor kissed.

So the conjecture is that even though my limbic system is unwinding, I'll retain my emotional memories for longer. It further turns out that these memories are profoundly associated with the sense of smell, and smell will continue to trigger them when much else has become unreachable. Did you see how she came into focus when I wrote "She smel swete like a flowr"? Apparently, the olfactory nerve, which conveys smell to the brain, is hotwired straight into your limbic system. It's a neural freeway, running wide and open direct to your deepest feelings. It'll take years to fade. I hope.

There are other smells as well, of course. I hope you're not easily offended. **When I smell her sex, it's as though my lust was first kindled** only yesterday.

Those deepest runnels of memory will unravel last of all. I'll forget who Lucia is, but I'll still love her.

So far, so good.

Love's redemptive qualities conquer all, as ever they did. The deeper the foundations, the stronger the edifice, as is so often the case. And, simply—*think positive*, as we frequently insist when confronted with adversity. Over and again we look to these homilies for support and, surprisingly, the evidence supports our reliance upon them. Literature, philosophy, science and myth all converge on the value of these charming yet practical notions.

Are they enough? Well... they work for me. They're a start. They're part of the developing composition of circumstances that are going to deliver me to the end of this story.

It's trite to describe the brain as an infinitely complex machine, but that's what it is. As complex on the biological scale as is the universe on the cosmological. Apparently, the phantom authority of quantum mechanics that pervades the universe also appears to influence the brain—in ways both perverse and counterintuitive. Some have gone so far as to speculate that consciousness itself is a product of quantum activity. They call it "orchestrated objective reduction." Astonishing, isn't it? I always imagined that mind was directed by self. But this theory implies that mind is derived from the random actions of subatomic particles. Or is it that these same particles dance to the tune of thought? Mind over matter? Or matter over mind?

Who really knows, or can ever know?

The trouble is, however you look at it, my mind's broke. But, by the grace of dumb luck, bad habits and genetic disposition—and no options—I seem to have stumbled on a solution. Yes, I have a plan. More accurately, Lucia and I have a plan. At the heart of our plan is the most outrageous proposition you'll have ever heard. That being the case, I'm banking on those sweet little notions I mentioned earlier, because they're the only part of the plan that make any sense.

OK. Let's get back to what you're thinking. Probably something along the lines of "He's got Alzheimer's, so how does all this work?"

Here we go.

I'm hoping you'll agree that what I'm doing, what I'm writing—right now—is fairly cogent, mostly rational. It might be right. It might be wrong. It might be wildly misguided, but it *hangs together*.

It's fundamentally different from the stunted words that I showed you previously. Reading those, you probably assumed that any dull glints of structure, or hint of serendipitous imagery, were just fumbled coincidence, stumbled upon by a mind clinging to some lingering strands of reason and self. Perhaps. Perhaps not.

In any event, you might reasonably be asking yourself, how does he do it? How can he suddenly switch like this? Like, for instance, now.

This is the complicated part.

My brain is gradually filling up with something called beta-amyloid. It's produced when a few poorly functioning genes begin to make a deformed version of something called the "amyloid precursor protein". Basically, this doesn't work properly and instead of regulating the beta-amyloid, it produces too much of it or makes it too sticky, or both. This gooey stuff bunches together forming clumps of toxic material called plaques. These plaques disrupt— and usually destroy—the brain cells which we rely on to think and act.

Part of the really difficult brain science is how this happens, but, at the very least, one of the main contenders is that the beta-amyloid causes the production of free radicals, poisonous substances which in turn cause something called oxidative stress. Here's the equation;

Free Radicals = Oxidative Stress = BAD.

Then you've heard of antioxidants right? Here's the other equation;

Antioxidants = less Free Radicals = GOOD.

So antioxidants are what we want. Lots of them. If we can concentrate them in our brain's own backyard, so much the better. Now, hold that thought because the next bit is about as counterintuitive as you'll ever come across. Here it is.

I live on a diet of cocaine and modafinil.

Again? Right.

I live on a diet of cocaine and modafinil. Controlled stimulants, to be clear. Worse still, from any conventional point of view, I've been taking coke for most of my adult life. Not an addict, exactly, but, you know, for fun. Recreational, I think they call it.

Despite all that you've ever heard or imagined, in certain circumstances coke has a strangely therapeutic effect.

It prevents my decline.

Really. Stay with me.

It was first noticed when certain laboratory rats were "challenged"—that's what the boffins call it—with significant doses of cocaine and amphetamine, for experimental purposes. Don't ask me why anyone would do this, but the effect was astounding: the rats produced a protein protecting them from the free radicals and oxidative damage the drugs would otherwise cause.

It turns out that these rats, and, crucially, some of us people, have a gene (or more precisely a gene transcript) which increases production of this protein precisely in response to such a challenge. The more drugs they gave them, the more protein they produced. The boffins christened it "Cocaine and Amphetamine Regulated Transcript," or CART for short.

No, honestly. Look it up.

The administration of either one of the drugs, or a combination in various proportions, "upregulated" (another boffin word, meaning "increased") the CART transcript to produce more of the CART protein. Under these conditions the lab rats produced it by the bucket load, as do the folks with the gene. And guess what: it's a powerful antioxidant. It's neuroprotective. And it's endogenous to the brain. It's made there.

I guess you can see where I'm going with this. If you take these drugs (and personally I only touch coke—at least it starts off as a leaf) *and* you've got the gene, you've got your own onboard antioxidant factory. You'll end up producing an environment in your head which is better able to withstand neurological damage.

It turns out that the same applies to modafinil. I discovered modafinil more recently courtesy of my poor sister who's got multiple sclerosis. It's described as "promoting wakefulness" and is also known to improve concentration and something called "working memory." Things you might value if you're losing them. She uses it to shrug off the crippling tiredness that accompanies the progression of her illness. Some of you might know modafinil as a "smart drug", like the one in the film called *Limitless*. No one knows quite how it works; certainly it affects another brain chemical called dopamine by preventing its absorption.

More dopamine equals more fun, more or less.

It shares that process with coke, if not quite with the same result. Modafinil also appears to activate a bunch of other biological systems that contribute to its effect. That's something the boffins haven't got their heads round—yet —but... the more the merrier, right?

Unlike coke, modafinil is not particularly addictive nor does it have any measurable side effects. But while coke only acts briefly, modafinil has got one of the longest half-lives in pharmacology. So, the coke pump-primes the antioxidant effect and modafinil picks up the baton and runs with it. And then just keeps on running.

Absurd? Beyond science fiction? Take a look at my notes in the postscript.

Anyway, the astoundingly useful side effect of this unconventional, unethical, untested, unproven and almost certainly unsafe cocktail therapy is that, for finite periods at least, I can think straight, see straight and even walk straight.

It's astonishing, and it's how I can switch. How I can do this.

Let's call it "Up."

Just for the puritans amongst you, modafinil is well known to reduce the euphoria associated with cocaine use. I'm not doing it for the buzz, I'm doing it to survive and when it's finished, I'm reduced to my bare bones. The bare bones of love and dependency.

Let's call that "Down."

So that's how it works. I've developed a regime that's keeping the Alzheimer's at bay, and which, when I'm "up", lets me think and act more or less normally. Oh, and *don't* try any of this at home, folks, because I have no idea what it would do to you.

I mean it.

Chapter Four

Lucia

My dad was from the Caribbean, from one of the Windward Islands—a small, mountainous country called St. Lucia, nestled between Martinique, St. Vincent, and Barbados. It's an old French colony, contested by the British for nearly two centuries, all for want of its sugar cane. Back and forth it went, changing hands over and again though the islanders barely noticed – let the foolish *étwanjé* exhaust themselves! After all this to-ing and fro-ing, St. Lucia finally gained its full independence on 22nd February 1979. The legacy of this merry-go-round is that they speak both English and French Creole, or "patois", which combines vocabulary derived mostly from French with syntax of African and Carib origin. The result is soft and lyrical like the music they play there.

My dad's name was Michel Richelieu. He was a proud St. Lucian, as am I, but neither the island's charm nor his pride in it could keep him there. Like many young Caribbean men of his day he answered the call from the "Mother Country" to come and help rebuild Britain—and London in particular—after the ravages of the Second World War. He arrived in the city in the mid-1950s, having secured an engineering apprenticeship at the London Hospital in the bombed and battered East End. Within ten years he was Head of Engineering, and that's where he stayed.

His original plan was to work in London for a few years and return to St. Lucia once he'd made his fortune, but it turned out my mother—who had initially stayed behind—had other ideas. Unlike my dad, she came from money and, back in those days, it was still quite fashionable—at least in the Windward Islands—to do the grand tour of Europe, like the Victorians had used to do. She convinced her own father to pay a little extra so she could visit my dad, in London, en route to Paris. That set the compass for the rest of their lives. My mother finished her tour, but instead of returning to St. Lucia, she came back to London.

She did not leave again.

I try to imagine how she saw things, back then. Why she traded her comfortable bourgeois life in St Lucia for the grime and graft of London's East End. There was my dad, of course. But she was also a much sought-after English teacher back home so, in her mind, my mother must have considered that she had means. But, once she settled in London she gradually found that her means were not means enough. The "Mother Country" was not as maternal as those optimistic emigrants had hoped, and black people had a difficult time of it. She soon became pregnant with my brother and sister and, later on, with me. Times were hard and my parents' nostalgia was strong, so they named me Lucia after their home.

My mother's time bearing me was extraordinarily difficult and she never properly recovered. Even so, she was persistent. After me, she endured two more pregnancies, the second of which provided her with the other son that she had always wanted. I was eight years old by then. It was the year I made my first communion. I have the only picture of me and my mother together; I in my communion gown, she in a sober suit, both of us unsmiling, our lips pressed tightly together. She died soon after. The dreams of my parents going back to St. Lucia together were over.

I still have our picture. I keep it on my nightstand and say a prayer for her every evening before I sleep.

My dad was crippled by her death and sank into the depths of an awful depression. I don't remember much from that miserable time; just that he was not the daddy I knew and wanted. Even though he forced himself to put on a brave front for *sé sala piti manmey*—the little children—he was sad, and lost.

Tragically, that was only the half of it.

He was a black man, seemingly alone, somehow working full time and with five kids to look after. So, aside from having to deal with the death of my mother, apart from his misery inside, apart from the unimaginable rigors of everyday life, he also had to fight the authorities who ordered that we five children be taken into care.

Torn from him, split up from each other and settled, one by one, elsewhere across the UK.

Could anything have been so cruel, or more wrong?

Fortunately, although he was in a dreadful state, my dad was *not* alone. He was enormously popular and had many friends amongst the nuns, priests and congregation of our church as well as the doctors and nurses at the hospital. These people rallied around him and with their references, practicalities, money and support he was eventually able to fight off the authorities and we were able to stay together. But it didn't stop there. My two elder sisters joined us from St. Lucia and with their help, and along with the help from his colleagues and from his wide network of friends in the church and Caribbean communities, my dad continued to take care of us. Disaster was averted.

By dint of his extraordinary determination, he instilled in us the values of pride and fortitude and the worth of hard work. He never let an opportunity pass to remind us that if our mother had been alive she would want us all to go to University and to hold good jobs.

To stand tall in our adopted country.

My dad saw to it that this was how it happened. One by one, we graduated and joined the British Civil Service, working for Her Majesty's Government. For a man of his generation, color and circumstance, it was all he could have ever asked.

His courageous, selfless nature is imprinted on us all. His dauntless spirit and fierce resolve in the face of such adversity has inspired us to be the best that we can, each and every day. When I hear, now, about the unfolding history of abuse in children's homes, back then and thereafter, it's clear that we dodged a dreadful bullet. My dad saved our lives and our mother was always by his side.

Growing up in the Richelieu household was a mixed bag, sweet and sour. My dad worked long hours to earn the money to feed and clothe five children, but he never complained.

He was a brilliant cook. He'd had to be—my mother had always been useless! He had a marvelous repertoire, and would cook the most amazing meals for us. Dried cod would soak for days, hydrating in bowls and saucepans. He'd have us slice goat and mutton into small cubes, and then he'd garnish it and pack it into containers to steep in the various exotic herbs and spices that reminded him of home. Strange vegetables like gnarled roots and spider's webs would be casually transmuted into delicious accompaniments. Our condiment rack grew and grew, gradually taking over the larder as friends and relatives came and went back and forth from the West Indies.

Patiently he taught all of his culinary tricks and devices to me and my sisters, though in my case the best I can say is that he tried. I was never a keen student in the kitchen. Of late, though, I have begun to acknowledge and embrace our culinary traditions. Curry goat has become my forte.

Now that I've someone to care for, yes, I am slowly beginning to enjoy cooking. It is an act of love. Look at me. I'm crying. I should have started earlier. First my dad, then Marc—they've both cooked for me all my life.

I wish I could have given it back. Sooner, when things were good.

My dad loved telling stories about growing up in St. Lucia. One of his most famous happened while he was courting my mum. At the time he had a small boat, which he used to ferry people around the island. St. Lucia is small and dotted with coastal towns. The interior is thick mountainous rain forest, so in those days it was quicker and cheaper to travel from one place to another by boat.

One day, so the story went, the prime minister was travelling from Castries to Vieux Fort for a *very important meeting*. Apparently his boat had broken down (the specifics were never mentioned) but my dad—and this part usually began in a hushed voice, gradually rising to a triumphant crescendo—was on hand to save the situation, miraculously fixing the boat with a nail, a piece of wire and some putty, thus getting the Prime Minister to his meeting *on time*.

Sometimes my mother was with him, naturally deeply impressed by his cool reactions, while at others she wasn't mentioned. Regardless, it seems the Prime Minister was so grateful to my dad that he subsequently invited to join him at his monthly game of dominoes.

We hung on his every word.

Much later, on one of my first solo visits to St. Lucia, I was walking along Vigie Beach near Castries. Out of nowhere, a middle-aged man came running up to me and said "You are Michael's daughter! I can tell!" The Richelieu genes are strong and we share many features and characteristics. Still, I was flabbergasted and said "Yes, I am," and introduced myself. He went on to tell me that my cousin lived just down the road from him and that he would tell him that I was here. I laughed and explained that I had already been in touch with him and that we were meeting up tomorrow.

The next day, my cousin took me out to dinner at the famous Green Parrot restaurant, overlooking Castries and the bay. The Caribbean Sea looked rich and warm, twinkling and shimmering under the setting sun. A soft breeze ruffled the crisp white table arrangements. Unasked but not unwelcome, the owner and chef came up to our table and talked for most of the evening about my dad and his adventures. The prime minister episode was duly noted. It seems my dad was still something of a legend, even then, so many years after he had left. Needless to say, our meal was on the house.

Once I grew up I realized exactly how much my dad had given up for us all. He never married again, even though he was a handsome man. He had a couple of girlfriends, later on, but he never brought them back to our house. He would have thought it improper.

When dad finally retired, he remained in London. I would visit him most days and we'd have long discussions about money, property (a great favorite), and the future. He taught me a lot about money—about finance and how to wield it, as well as the canny tricks of a black man far from home. This I have put to good use.

I loved chatting with him, gradually putting together the pieces of his history. I think he had a hard upbringing, and then a hard life, but he never showed a trace of bitterness.

Still, he was lonely, and towards the end of his life he would chat to me about my mother, something he never did while I was growing up. Nor did he ever reveal how proud he was of us but we found out, after his death, that he constantly talked about us to his friends, his colleagues and the nuns and the priest of St. Michaels, our church. So I guess he was proud. He didn't say it for fear of making us complacent. Complacency had no part in his life.

My great regret is that my dad wasn't able to see me marry. He always said he was looking forward to walking me down the aisle. On his deathbed Marc leaned over him and promised to always look after me. I feel certain that he heard it and died in that knowledge.

I just hope he is looking down on us now, as I hope he was when we were walking down the aisle on 10th April, all those years ago.

It's about Marc and me now.

Chapter Five

Marc

I see you've met Lucia. She's awesome, no? Luminous, gracious, gorgeous and possessed of a reserve of spiritual depth and commitment that I fundamentally lack. I didn't realize the extent to which these qualities were absent in me until I met her. And now, I don't mind because she has enough for us both. I draw on her like a vampire—probably more often than I should, though I doubt that she even notices.

I see you've also met her Daddy. I sometimes think I'm just the follow-on, the support act, a pale imitation of his towering presence in her life—but not so often that it bothers me. And anyway, she's always been worth every scintilla of effort and energy that I've been able to offer in homage to her poise, charm, and beauty.

And all that she does for me.

She's not just sweetness and light though. I told you she was from the London's East End, didn't I? It's a hard place anyway, and growing up there, a black girl—the daughter of West Indian immigrants in the sixties and seventies—burnished her with a patina of toughness and street-smarts that she employs instinctively and ruthlessly if threatened. Like a lioness, dreaming, relaxed, but alert.

Anyway, where was I?

I'm going down. My time's running out for today. I can feel the familiar, insidious fog condensing at the fringes of my mind. Then again, perhaps it's more akin to the subtle trespass of absolute zero: at first colonizing, then petrifying my increasingly fragmentary thoughts. I watch one, a single thought—momentarily clear and lucid, but it quickly turns to frozen crystal and then frosts over until it blurs. I lose sight of it and it slips away. Can I reach it?

No.

This is how the struggle begins.

Let me try and show you what it's like to be bound by the glacial delirium of dementia. Thoughts only form in turn—the glimpse of an image, or the chime of a word or sound, perhaps even the resonance of feeling. Each component is sequentially and meticulously conjured with exquisite, painstaking determination until I can focus upon its content. It's a myth to say that Alzheimer's dims and dulls our thinking. Each thought, when I can cling long enough to it, is perfect in its manifestation—like a Hilliard miniature, or a CAD blueprint. Too often, though, the effort to retain these fleeting zephyrs requires more energy than I can muster. Imagine the enormity of sustaining this thought while simultaneously striving to divine the next so as to join them together to make an idea. For me, it's both akin to and on the scale of nuclear fusion; the summoning of vast energies—the kindling of stars—to begin the chain reaction. If I can achieve this I'll sometimes be rewarded with a cascade of thoughts—fluid, iridescent streamers and cartwheels that spin and concatenate until I feel dizzy with sentience. The problem then is their articulation.

Set against this peculiar ebb and flow—more ebb than flow, to be sure—the world is strangely relativistic, tightly but inversely geared to the frequency of my thinking. When I'm focused on that single act, the world flickers by in a flurry of incoherent images like random cuts from an abstract movie. Conversely, when the reaction starts the world presents itself as a collection of frozen frames; silent static panes of plate glass daubed with life-size stills of the people and objects around me.

I think I glean some meaning from both these states. Occasionally, afterwards, I find I've gained some ground.

I was talking about Lucia, wasn't I? That wasn't what I wanted to say. No, wait, I wanted to say it but it wasn't the point of this chapter. I've been wandering. It was a good point though. It framed her as someone formidable in adversity.

It's late. The modafinil is wearing thin and I'm going to need some more coke if I'm going to finish this. Please, bear with me a moment.

As I said earlier, the deepest and strongest neural links are the last to go. That must apply to my motor neurons as well because even as the veil creeps towards me I can still fix myself up. It's a well-worn routine, no doubt profoundly reinforced by my dopamine reward circuits—probably the strongest connections of all. Instinctive, almost.

First of all, I dissolve the pure, pearlescent white powder in distilled water. Out of habit, I drop an unnecessary piece of clean cotton wool into the solution to act as a filter. I crack open a fresh hypodermic and suck up the clear, clean liquid. The sequence accelerates to its finale as I savor the sharp sting of the fine surgical steel, the bloody crimson flower blooming in the barrel, the firm straight shot of the plunger.

And I breathe again.

Don't worry, it's unadulterated. We're sort of wealthy and have, ummm, professional connections. It's not from the street and I take modest, fixed doses.

Lucia doesn't like doing it for me, though she will if she must.

I'm sorry for the rambling. Sort of an occupational hazard now. All I wanted was to summarize how things are for me right now. Just briefly, because sleep beckons.

My drug use, distasteful though it may be to most—if not all—of you, stimulates a powerful antioxidant buffer against the ravages of the Alzheimer's beta-amyloid infestation. Disabled, deactivated, and dysfunctional my brain cells may be, but they're *not dead yet*.

Mercifully, the many tests I've had to submit to have demonstrated that, touch wood, so far there doesn't appear to be any manifestation of the very scary tau protein "neurofibrillary tangles", which spell certain progression to the end game.

You don't tangle with the tangles.

So that's good.

Fortunately, not to say miraculously, for me at least the use of these drugs is as rousing as it is therapeutic. This means I can use my craft and cunning to plot and plan a better outcome.

To fix me we have to do two things: clear out the amyloid plaques, and then re-boot the neurons. How difficult can it be? OK, it's really quite difficult. But. There are two cutting edge therapies that promise to do just this: Alpha-Mabetamine and Limenofil-X7 respectively. They work. Well, they work in mice. And they don't hurt humans. *And* they're ready to test. I just have to find out where and how to get them.

Though I look forward to the recovery of my poor numb nerves in due course, in the meantime—unless I'm properly dosed—I'm pretty much just another miserable, early-onset Alzheimer's victim.

That's it for now. A few more things we've got to pick up next time but I think we're mostly through the background. Soon we'll get on to the story.

Good night, God bless, sleep tight.

Chapter Six

The Inhibitionist

Pane. Tierd. Fink bad
nowe. Th. Thiink bad.
Lushcia say 'fink'. Got
her teef on he r lip,
cockney stile.
Halo its me agane. Slo
in the morning. Or
weneva itis. She give
me tablit orreddy
alreddy so be kwiq
soone.
No not giv me tabblit
yet. Sta slo. Cant
rimembr
Funy thing is I remembr
far back wen slo. Can
be good becorse all gon
uther times.

Aneyway. Thiink bad but thiink thinking sumthing from long a go. Must wrihgt it down becorse forget else.
Think this:
Meny yeres a go werked in govornament. In siense sience. Gon get this rihgt. Looke itup.
Caled BIOTECHNOLOGY.
Speld it rihgt.
BIOTECHNOLOGY.
Takes long makes tierd me.
Must get rigt too.
Wuman hoo grate frend.
Looke itup two too.
Here...
Donna Fulbright.
Importnt. Big wuman.
biG like boss. sHe kno

sientests.   Speshally abowt
kno this know this dam
mus lookit up
Spechally abotw
ALZHEIMRS.
Ther.   Writ   it   down.
None noon no one els
kno.   Nor   lusha   but
donna stil alive and
kno most and best abowt
it abowt peopl whoo can
fix it.
Reel   tierd   now   want
tablet.
See? Tablet. Not stupd.
Things somtimes clear.

Chapter Seven

Lucia

Dear God, hello, it's Lucia. I hope you are listening, especially today. And I hope mum and Dad are with you because I need all of your help. I mean all of you as well as all you can give me.

First, I'm sorry I thought the worst of Linda when we spoke yesterday. I know she has her troubles but they seemed pale compared with mine and I just thought she was a selfish bitch without care or compassion. She wouldn't listen when I most needed her to. But all troubles are relative and we live in the middle of our own where we feel them most and deepest. I shouldn't judge. So please... look after her.

And I'm sorry I wished ill on Marc's boys. They help all they can but they have their own lives and families and it would be wrong to neglect them, and it is wrong of me to demand more or harbor contempt for their motives or envy for their freedom. Please look after them and theirs.

Dad, are you well? I need your strength. You looked after mum when she was ill and all of us after she'd gone. How did you do it? Where did you find the resolve, the stamina, the sheer will to survive?

I feel that everything is falling apart now. I need that strength.

God, I always thanked you for bringing Marc into my life. After all those years of waiting for him to work out his intentions—years of pain I might add—and years during which I never lost faith that we would be together. Sometimes I wondered, though, whether the spark that you lit in us both had sputtered out in him, whether it was still smoldering or if his ex-wife had managed to extinguish it completely with her black magic. I thought all these things but underneath it all I held tight to my hope. And you made me right.

For all those years after, I thanked you every night for the joy and fulfillment I felt with Marc in my life. Joy in the heart of me, the still, quiet sort of joy that renders everything serene and enables you to stand on your own two feet and always face the world. And then that other kind of joy—the heady, crazy whirlwind of love as we seemed to zoom around the world—Paris, Berlin, Brussels, New York, Washington, Los Angeles, Miami, Las Vegas, in floating palaces on the high seas, in our houses in London and America and, oh God, all the wonderful sex we had in all of those places. Dizzy, wonderful passionate, dirty sex where anything and everything was permitted and nothing was off limits.

I thanked you every night for all of it.

Then came the first faltering of his being. The tiny stutters of faulty memory. The faint forgetfulness, unattributable, and mostly inconsequential. The pauses as he sought a word. He always had words. Words for everything. Words I'd never heard, which he would then patiently explain, guiding me through the labyrinth of his thoughts. Sometimes they were difficult thoughts, long and complex, sometimes dark. I'd think he was depressed, such was their sinister cast but he'd laugh and say that there was nothing new under the sun. There was nothing he'd thought or was thinking that hadn't been thought before, and that anyway these ideas were trivial shadows when set besides my light and life. That made me feel good. Great, even.

Then the words died. And the thoughts diminished, and he could no longer explain them or even finish them. By then I knew something was going wrong. So we had the tests and then they said it.

"We're sorry, Mrs. Russell. Your husband has early stage Alzheimer's."

After the diagnosis, we both went a bit crazy. Drinking, fucking, spending money like we were trying to compress life into a day. I suppose it was classic denial. Marc, being Marc, drifted further and further towards the drugs, something I'd hoped I had helped to put behind him over the years. We tarried a while with rage and frustration but soon discovered how destructive they were and we quickly left them alone. Mercifully, we didn't direct them against one another. Then, as sure as night follows day, despondency soon followed destruction. Despondency was the worst. Coupled with the appalling apathy that the disease imparts, we slumped deeper and deeper into a state of miserable submission. There was no light anymore.

Dear God, why did you kindle, foster and cultivate our love only to do this to us? To rob us of all you granted? I can't imagine anything crueler. I try to summon a reason, or divine your purpose, but I confess there is nothing that lends itself to my imagination. Nothing that justifies these mysterious ways that you have laid upon us. Forgive me— I had to say these things because they are in my heart and to leave them there, well, I'm sure they'd turn to poison and pollute my faith and my hope. So God, now I've sucked on it—now I've spat it out—I feel a little better. Better enough to discuss the future perhaps. Certainly better enough to measure where we're up to.

So where is that?

We're fighters, Marc and I. He soon noticed the step change that his devil's cocktail of modafinil and cocaine had on his ability to be and to do. As you know, he's always dabbled in these things; this just meant he became systematic about them. Supplies, processes, schedules, equipment and oh, the reading and research, the conjectures and questions. He found out about the CART gene and its ability to protect his brain's neurons and synapses. Gradually he has built a case in his mind: that if he can but dispel those sinister deposits in his brain, if he can somehow flush them away, his nerves will bounce back and we can return to our wonderful life.

I flutter, like a trapped butterfly, between this vision as my hope and this vision as my final, crushing damnation as everything collapses in tears and failure. I would tend more to the latter were it not for three things: first, there really is mounting evidence that this gene, when strongly stimulated, has remarkably protective powers; second, that experimental drugs now exist to rid the body of the broken amyloid that causes the trauma; and third, that a substance has been created to fortify and revivify the afflicted cells— in some of God's creatures, at least.

There is another thing. As far as we can tell, there is nobody else on this earth who manifests the response that Marc does to his regimen of stimulants. His clarity of mind and will—when so medicated—is stronger even than I remember. So what is going on? Perhaps he's right, and that in the end it's just a freak of genetic luck. And that, by the same token, all of his other strange ideas might also prevail.

It really is our only light and, with him, I will reach for it.

But God... God... hear me. I hate the drugs. Now I will say your prayer and then I too must sleep.

"Our Father who art in Heaven,
Hallowed be thy name;
Thy kingdom come
Thy will be done
On earth as it is in heaven.
Give us this day our daily bread;
And forgive us our trespasses
As we forgive those who trespass against us;
And lead us not into temptation,
But deliver us from evil.
For thine is the Kingdom.
The power and the glory

For ever and ever,

Amen."

Chapter Eight

Marc

After we got my results, after we'd processed them, after we'd railed and rallied but before I'd discovered my—how shall I put it—alternative therapy, we resolved to try every avenue in pursuit of a cure. At first I think it was all about building a barrier against hopelessness: there is, after all, no known treatment for dementia. Thus our attention turned to where hope might yet spring eternal. The frontier. The leading edge of medical science where things are not known to have failed, where things might yet work. So we spoke to the doctors and discovered that there is an entire infrastructure, a subculture even, of people—researchers, patients, and practitioners—all engaged at the weird fringes of human pathology, thinking the unthinkable, pushing the envelope, innovating and testing, winning and losing.

The place where they all meet is the stage one clinical trial, the bow wave of hope for the driven and the desperate. Sometimes these trials succeed, but more often they fail. Many participants have died, either because the treatment they were testing failed or, in some cases, because it killed them. Some—a few—survive. Cured, against all the odds. Typically the successes are marginal but occasionally—rarely—they provide spectacular breakthroughs.

This, then, is my conviction: that I can be amongst them.

My diagnosis was made four years ago, and it's been two years since we pulled ourselves together enough to start investigating our way out of it. I signed up for everything available at first, without insight or acumen. I'd have travelled to Bogota or Brisbane if it had meant *doing* something, but it was like being an unknown actor on the casting couch: "I'm sorry, Mr. Russell, your condition is too advanced; I'm sorry Mr. Russell, your condition isn't advanced enough; I'm sorry but you're too young; you're too old; we're targeting this that or the other ethnic group; your blood's the wrong sort..." The reviews were poor, the rejection notices piled up. Jesus, who'd be a guinea pig?

As my fanatical, obsessive voyage of discovery progressed, I gradually focused my attention on the "flush and fix" regime that I've already mentioned. There are a number of institutions pursuing this approach, each using different drugs and combinations of drugs. Any would have done, back then, as far as assuaging my hope was concerned.

None of them accepted me. But, as Lucia often says: "It all happens for a reason." And who am I to argue with that?

The reason turned out to be that I eventually uncovered the work of an obscure Algerian academic called Algernon Benacerrafi. He'd published a paper in which he claimed to have established and perfected the process for combining Mabetamine and Limenofil. As I burrowed my way through the literature I realized that, without any hype or fanfare, a clinical trial of his cocktail was being commissioned. It was being coordinated by an organization called the Micklethwaite Foundation, a small charitable trust with a toehold in St. Bartholomew's Hospital.

St. Barts! That's where I'm registered! Lucia, too. Five miles as the crow flies makes it, literally, our local hospital. Why hadn't they told us? Why weren't we informed? We signed up.

We were too late.

"Marc we've got to—"

"It's not going to work."

"—go and see the doctors—"

"It's not going to work Lucia."

"—and ask them to let you join—"

"The clinical trials probably already begun—"

"—yes. The clinical trial."

"—and they won't take on a straggler. It'll skew the results. We're too late."

"But Marc, they're good people, they won't only be thinking about their outcomes. They'll respond to us. Really."

I look at her, kind of astounded at her conviction.

"Lulu, I just don't believe that. Do you believe it? I looked at the trial announcement, its specification and I tracked down the budget. At least the part of it they were willing to publish. This is a big deal, for all that nobody fucking mentioned it." I spat the words out. "Probably the biggest Alzheimer's breakthrough yet. I don't know how we missed it, for fuck's sake. The doctors aren't good people. They're functionaries on the inside of an institution. And we're not. We're on the outside. The wrong side."

"But look at all they did for me." A while back she'd had a small operation at St. Barts. It was a great success. The staff were superb. She considers this for a moment, realizes its irrelevance, then worries: "Do you think it was my fault? Should I have demanded more? Looked harder?"

"Lulu... Lucia. Darling. Don't take it on yourself. We've chased down every lead. They missed us out, one way or the other. As for your treatment – it was routine. Routine surgery, for a common problem. In, fix it, out. Of course they were nice. They *are* nice, I grant you. But it was a job. The drug trial is a different ballgame. It's the start of tsunami of money, if it works out. There's no room for random compassion. Or random people."

"But we were all signed up to the Clinical Trial Exchange! We're registered there. They knew all about you. Well, not *all* about you. Not about this." She waves vaguely. She's talking about the drugs. "You're a puzzle. I thought they'd be interested. I thought they had a duty."

Lucia looks crestfallen, distraught. She believes firmly and faithfully in the essential goodness of our health service, even now, despite the latter day onslaught of cuts and privatizations. Of course; she grew up in a family whose core ethic was derived from the Great British National Health Service. It provided employment, subsidized housing, preferential benefits and pensions; it provided exemplary care and an abiding sense of community for the tapestry of migrant folk, newly arrived—by express invitation—here on our dour islands, from Britain's global network of colonial territories and dependencies. It provided her care as a poor child, support during the years after her mother died and a sense of continuity forever since. She mourns the loss of all those things, vexing at the politicians who would cut it, then cut it again.

But this is the first time it's actually failed her. I suppose it must feel something like grief.

On the other hand, I've rarely used our national treasure and even more rarely needed it. I come from a medical family, and an unusually vigorous one at that. On the odd occasions any of us were ever ill we were whisked through a series of friends, colleagues, and contacts to a consultant or professor who would dispatch us to some leafy clinic replete with batteries of science fiction-grade medical equipment, therapies, and drugs. The treatment was swift and mechanical. Job done. My faith leant naturally towards the empirical, the practical, and the pragmatic.

It's not that I don't trust our health service, exactly; it's just that I've barely thought about it. If I have, I suppose I've felt a sense of distant and probably diffident trust. This was a mistake. Not that Lucia's wrong. The people who work for the NHS appear, still, against all the odds, to be dedicated and diligent, committed and compassionate, and, above all capable and clever. The trouble is this: there are too few of them and too many of us. Whether by accident or design they'd all passed us by.

And so here we are. At the first hurdle. Teetering on the point of failure.

"We've got to sort it out," Lucia says, and from the tone of her voice and set of her mouth that is, inevitably and precisely, what we're going to do. "I'll phone them, now, and talk to them."

"Lucia, before you do that, let's think a minute. What do we want from them? What can they offer us? Unless we're clear, this isn't going to help."

"We want to get you on the trial. That's it."

"You know we can't just phone up and demand that. Who do we know best there? I mean, who do *you* know best?"

The truth is I barely know anybody. We've decided not to tell them about my drug regime. For good reason. Obviously it's illegal, for starters. Then, if they decided there was something in it, I expect I'd be sequestered away in some high security facility somewhere with no hope of reaching my ends. I'm basically a private, no—make that paranoid—individual and I don't want anyone else involved, end of story. The upshot of this is that whenever I see my consultants, I don't do the drugs, so I don't know my arse from my elbow.

"We should see Professor Gaynes. He's sweet, and he's weak." She is so ingenuously calculating.

"OK. So maybe we should ask for a clinical review, and then use the meeting to broach the trial? We—you—need to be face to face with him. Agreed?"

"Agreed," she nods. Our accord is one of faith. Mine is pragmatic. Lucia's is existential, spiritual and mysterious. As is so often the case, these opposing tides continue to bear us in the same direction. No sooner are we decided than we're ready to move on. "Yes, that's better. I can do that. I'll speak to his secretary. We get on."

Lucia has spoken. Consider it done. Without pause she reaches for the phone. She's put through, switches the phone to speaker and I listen as she goes to work.

"Hi Paula, this is Lucia…Lucia Russell. Remember the Christmas cake? How are you?" Christmas cake? What Christmas cake? When? She continually astounds me with her endless surprises, all the small bridges built.

"Mrs. Russell, Lucia, of course—I'm fine." Paula's voice sounds warm, responsive. I can't even remember who she is. "Of course I remember, yes. The cake was lovely. Thank you. How are you? And how's Marc? What can I do for you?" So much stuff going on and I have no idea. Was it always like this, before? Maybe it was. These are Lucia's gifts.

"Oh, you know, I'm fine—bearing up. Marc's so-so. That's why I'm calling, actually. Paula, I wonder if you can help. Could you possibly book Marc an appointment with Professor Gaynes? It's been a while since we had a review and it would be great if he could fit us in! And I've got a few new questions I'd like to ask."

"Of course, Lucia, that should be OK. Tell me— when was the last time you both came in?"

"Ummm—it was some time ago, we came by but only for blood tests. Ah—do you remember when we last spoke? It was a couple of months ago—we bumped into each other in the canteen."

"Oh right, yes, hang on..."

She's not really listening as she searches for a time and date to accommodate us. Lucia looks over at me while we listen to the amplified stutter of her keyboard as Paula logs into her terminal, clicking rapidly through to her journal. It sounds like gunfire.

"OK, yes, I've got it. Here we are. Lucia, when's best for you? We've got a free appointment next week. Nine a.m., Tuesday. It's an early one but it's soon. I keep them for the good 'uns. That's you."

"That is fantastic, Paula, I am soooo grateful." Lucia draws out her words as she seals the deal. "Brilliant. No need to send out an appointment— we'll be there. I'll just put it in my phone..."

"Well, I shouldn't worry—the system sends out the appointment anyway. You'll get it in a day or two. Look, we'll see you and Marc next week. It's probably best if he doesn't eat breakfast. We might have to run some more tests, just routine."

No, I won't be eating. I won't be doing any drugs either. This is going to be Lucia's show. I shall remain mute. Effortlessly playing the fool.

"Paula, thanks again. Really. See you then, have a lovely day. Bye."

Lucia puts the phone down and smiles slightly over at me. "Now let's see," she says, inscrutably.

Chapter Nine

Marc and Lucia

Marc

Maybe you've noticed there's very little reference to time in this narrative. No sense of day, nor night. Nor even of time passing. That's because we're on my time. Drug time. Or Alzheimer's time. Neither case cares much for the quantum tick and the finite tock.

When I'm up, I'm up for the duration, chemical clockwork blindly unwinding on a schedule that registers the circadian rhythms and rhymes of neither the sun nor the moon.

When I'm down, I'm down. I don't recognize or register much at all, except in the deepest fissures of my being.

So, when you consider how superfluous time has become, it seems unnecessary to invoke it as a means of chronicling events, or even organizing these words. Sometimes, say when it seems like it's just me talking to you, Lucia might be asleep. That might be at 7pm, or it might be midday. Other times, when Lucia and I are talking to each other, or we're planning and plotting, it could just as easily be 3am. So. We'll make a deal. If it's important, or if I remember, I'll try and mention it occasionally—for the record, as it were. Other than that, it's probably just best to assume that the events I'm describing are more or less consecutive, just like in real life.

No doubt it's been difficult for Lucia, adapting to my peculiar ebb and flow, but we seem to have developed a pattern. Some things we have to do when the rest of the world does them. Other things we do when our rhythms coincide.

Like now, for instance. We both want sex. It's 11:27am, just for the record.

I shut the blinds and our bedroom is suddenly dark, the shadows intensified by the thin, bright shafts of sunlight that slice through the slim blades of aluminum. I lie back, propped regally on a gantry of pillows and cushions covered in crisp white cotton and intricate lace. I had some extra cocaine before we began and I'm tumescent.

I grasp myself as you kneel over me. Watching you slide your pretty G-string aside, I squeeze hard, rubbing a little. Some liquid seeps out and I catch it on my finger and shine your nipple. You look down and breathe in deeply, nostrils flaring. Your nipple grows visibly and your hips thrust forward.

"Stop it," you say, regaining control. "Get back to holding it. Don't touch me. Hold it firm, and then we can continue."

I do as you say and you straddle my hips. You reach down and some juice gets on your finger, yours I think though I'm not sure. You lean forward and invite me to lick it off. I do and you give me a dirty smile, then part your lips and expose your pearl, gleaming and rosy with lust. You press it against me and start to rotate your hips in tiny circles.

"Don't move," you admonish, as I start to jerk upwards, "keep your arse still, you're all mine." You reach down and grip me. "It's my toy," you croon, "and it's for my pleasure." You play a while then you wriggle, impatiently. "I want it bigger. Let me touch your nipples." You squeeze them, hard, then warn: "but you still can't move." You close a gentle hand around my bollocks then give a sharp squeeze. "If you do, I'll squeeze much harder."

So I lie there, lust coursing through my body, your sweet ministrations bringing me to bursting point. Likewise, I can see you're getting ready to come. You lay your forefingers on your labia and push the lips back so your nub stands proud, pink and hard. Small, tight, intense movements herald your orgasm, and just as you start to climax you jam yourself firmly down on me, wriggling and grinding as your womb relaxes so that it feels like you've sucked me up to the very hilt.

After a long sigh you're ready. "You can come now, but I want to watch. I want to see it." We change places and I kneel beside you "I'm going to squeeze your nipples hard," you purr, "and you can only move your hand around the top. Yes, that's nice, fast and tight, beat it off, you're ready I can tell. Look at those big things, they're bursting. So are you ready? I am. Come on, I'm ready now. Cover me in it."

I love to hear your lust. As I listen to your words I can feel the pressure build, the tiny hard movements of my hand bringing a slow but extreme orgasm to a head.

When I can no longer hold it back I let go and we both watch the spasms of thick semen splashing over the rich caramel flesh of your breast as I pump it out. It drips down and over onto your sweet belly. We rest a moment before we start over.

Lucia

I'm squatting over his shoulders, looking down at his handsome shaft which is standing up rigid from his abdomen. Both his groin and his balls are shaven and smooth. They looked succulent. I'm curious to see what else the cock can do so I try tweaking his erect nipples—a guaranteed stimulant I've long and joyfully employed—which are just visible between my thighs. To my delight it jerks upwards, pointing nicely at my breasts. I squeeze them again and it seems to visibly grow as more of his hot blood flows into it. A third time and a fresh drop of clear juice emerges from the tip. I can feel myself drawn towards it, almost unconsciously making an "O" of my lips. I make a circle with my fist and start to rub him and I'm quickly rewarded by the gentle rotation of his hips. This looks nice, like I've still got him well in control. A little pull here, and he'll do this. A squeeze there and he'll do that.

Very good.

Am I perverse? I don't think so. What woman doesn't love this power over her man? Doesn't revel in it. I shift my arse a little, fitting myself more firmly against his mouth. He gasps a little, then starts breathing more deeply as his tongue continues its work. I move my body forward and down, taking care not to disrupt his blandishments. He takes his hands off my hips and his fingers find my ripe nipples. Very delicately he takes each one between his thumb and middle finger and begins to brush the erect flesh with his forefingers. The sensation is quickly overwhelming and suddenly I'm beginning to feel less objective, moving my hips with more instinctive purpose and less control. I can feel his cock sliding urgently between my tits. It's slippery with come.

But then my need takes over. Suddenly I get up. "You're not wasting that. I want it in me. I want it all." I turn around and kneel, back dipped, arse high, poised before his urgent desire. I look back over my shoulder. He's staring down at me as if unsure what to do next. But he's sure. He pulls up to the bumper, pauses a moment and then goes the whole way. I imagine him watching, his eyes fixed on our conjunction. He holds my hips loosely and starts moving, languorous at first, slowing things down. Each time he withdraws he waits a second or two, barely maintaining his presence inside me. That's fine with me. I enjoy the sweet suspense of it. For a while he appears content to keep it leisurely, gliding sensuously back and forth, occasionally stroking my back with his fingertips.

But it can't last. Our restraint erodes and he begins to pick up the pace. Leaning forward he cradles my breasts, gradually focusing on my nipples again, now teasing, now squeezing. Unable to help myself, I begin to drive myself back towards him, meeting and matching his increasingly potent thrusts. He shifts his hands and grips my hips tightly, taking control. My internal muscles relax completely and I feel consumed by his sex as he slides further into the core of me. I buck wildly as I start to come, grinding my arse against his groin as my lust runs over.

Suddenly he pulls out, manhandling me onto my back, then pulling me towards him. Again he looks down at me for a second, feasting his eyes. He doesn't wait long though. He lifts my buttocks towards him and slips himself up inside me then leans over, resting on his elbows as he bends to kiss me, hard and passionate. On an impulse, I reach down his back, over his working buttocks and squeeze his arse, moving it to match my own rhythm. God, it feels good. And now I'm coming again. I want us to come together. His arse begins its last frenetic thrusting, forcing him even further into me. "Fuck me, hard, empty your balls, give me all of it," I demand as his juice boils over. He looks straight into my eyes while I take his orgasm, spasm after spasm as his loins thrust and dance until he's drained. I drink in the delicious intimacy, feeling as if I'm tasting him with my naked womb.

Marc

We lie together for a while. The shafts of sunlight gradually shift across the floor and up onto the bed. The frontrunner illuminates our toes. I can feel that I will soon be going down, into hibernation. I tell Lucia that it's time. She begins to cry.

"I'm sorry," she says, rubbing her eyes. "It's so hard doing this, it's like constantly saying goodbye. I don't mind looking after you, I don't even mind administering the drugs. It's watching you go away." She sits up, her arms hugging her knees.

"My dear, I'm sorry. You know I don't go away, you're always in my heart. I still know you. You've seen my little notes. You're the light. Then just as now."

"Yes I know, I know. Still, it's hard. I suppose it's having to constantly adapt. I'm always off balance. I want one person, not two."

"Which one do you want? One's easy. We just give up. But if you want me like this—me, the real me," I speak more vehemently than I intended, then calm myself, "this version—then we have to keep going. We have to push on."

"Of course I want you to be like this. But I want it to be because you're better, not because you're pumped full of drugs." I sigh and stroke her back for a while. We've come to believe there can be an outcome. Now it's about limits and limitations.

There are only two questions left, really.

How far must we go? (How far will I go? How far can you go?)

And...

What lines must we cross?

Chapter Ten

The Inhibitionist

Want mor sex wiv her.
Cunt. Mene cant. can't.
Canot do it. Want but
but
but wat? sHy. I shY. No
cunt. Can't.
Go to docters sune.
Speke wit they abowt
me. I lost in here.
Must make ill go awa.
Sad sad
Lusha wil make vem do
ritghte do gud for me.
But not all.
Not byvemselvs. Must
rmember biote bitec
bology biotecnogology
wuman but cant

Wont go work wolk. No.
try bettr. I wanto go
Owt. I go owt for wolk.
Dark owt bu t I not
fritend.
Trese bloeing in big
winde. Coled. Coled on
mey fete Coled onmy
fase. Big brigte litght
push no shine at me.
Car.
Man put me incar. Go
howm he say. We go.
Lucsha cry TeeRs. Wher
my abybe baybe go she
cry.
Hold me tite.

Chapter Eleven

Marc and Lucia

Marc

Well. That was a disaster: unmitigated chaos and catastrophe from beginning to end, courtesy of Yours Truly. Lucia will have to tell you the greater part of the story because I was, unwittingly, beyond control or reason: a calamitous buffoon. I ran amok through wards, rampaged through operating rooms and caused pandemonium, anger and a kind of grim, horrified hilarity among the gathered medics, patients and administrators of the august and historic St. Bartholomew's Hospital, rooted deep in the ancient parish of Spitalfields, old London Town.

It was awful.

In 1918, Norman Moore, Fellow of the Royal College of Physicians, wrote in his History of St Bartholomew's Hospital: *"If anyone should go into the hall at about twenty minutes past nine, he would see some hundred persons standing in an orderly manner, trying to look as if they were not pushing towards the various exits and entrances, and some four hundred others ranged on the forms; the women engaged in conversation, the men waiting in silence. If he goes out and comes in again at eleven, he will frequently find the room nearly or quite empty."*

It didn't work like that for me.

I'm talking about the occasion of our appointment with Professor Gaynes—admirably negotiated by Lucia and now been and gone. We'd had a plan. We'd debated our tactics long and hard, going around and around the possibilities but always returning to, and once more acknowledging, the simple central fact: I want on the trial.

If I've contrived to preserve and sustain my precious ganglia so far, well—it won't last forever. I need to flush the garbage in my head.

So we'd concentrated on how to clinch that. It boiled down to nothing better than charm and money.

Gaynes may or may not be weak, as Lucia reckons, but he's certainly in thrall to her. Fancies her, probably. It dawns on me, even as I write, that perhaps this is precisely what she means by being weak; less weakness *per se*, but rather his weakness for her, something which she will have divined and calibrated to a fine point. In any event, we'd reasoned that if charm wasn't going to cut it, we'd shift to cash.

And we'd go all in.

Did I mention we were well off? Comfortable, not rich; we can wager fifty thousand, more if necessary. So if Lucia were to feel our chance was slipping away she would offer an endowment, or a gift... or a bribe, whatever she deemed best suited to delivering the art of the possible. It would leave some for us—or Lucia at least—to live on afterwards, if the worst comes to the worst. But not a lot.

As plans go, it wasn't much. It depended on an awful lot of assumptions, had little scope, and lacked contingency.

Not that it mattered, because it was doomed from the start.

I remember the crowds. Luminous blotches of humanity ebbing and flowing against the stark backdrop of a clinically white facade punctuated by shimmering slabs of glass and steel. I remember the coiled worms of anxiety writhing in my gut and the gathering fear pressing on my skull. I remember the momentary lull as Lucia's warm presence enfolded the man we sat with, her caramel tones softening his spikes and edges. I remember the explosion of grief and pain and anguish as I heard the cacophonous noise of words I didn't understand but which lacerated my ears, then seared my dim consciousness.

I remember the frozen frames of my flight through the hospital; faces that laughed, fingers that pointed, mouths that shouted and screamed. There was a bland door with some blinking letters above it. There was a body with its bowels open to the world, flesh set aside like a hotel duvet, blank masked faces scaring me backwards, away, away. I remember falling metal and grabbing hands, a scalpel protruding from my thigh, and running, always running.

Eventually the remembering stopped and everything went black instead.

In 1737 William Hogarth, probably the world's best known pictorial satirist and social critic, painted 'Christ by the Pool of Bethesda' for Governors of St. Bartholomew's. He did it for free, a charitable work for a charitable institution. It's a huge picture—fully thirty feet across—and still hangs in the North Wing's Great Hall. It shows Christ healing the sick in bucolic surroundings with a watchful angel overhead. On closer scrutiny, though, each of the secondary figures in the painting is beset by grotesque ailments, a bizarre twist that belies Hogarth's nod to the classical form and instead substitutes a surreal vision of a dystopian asylum.

Now, why would I mention that?

"**B**ut that's it. That's all I can remember." I'm raking over the debacle at the hospital, desperate to come to terms with what, it turns out, appears to be a terminal situation as far as our – my – diminishing hopes are concerned. It's the day after. I'm dosed up and fizzing with a sense of incipient panic. Lucia and I are sitting together at home over coffee, so apparently normal, though I have a bandage on my thigh and my leg hurts. I'm thinking hard, trying but struggling to ride the wave of foreboding that threatens to engulf me, but I've run into a wall; no recollection, no insight. I've got nothing.

"Lucia, what happened? What went wrong?"

"Calm Marc, calm. Breathe. Slow down. We'll go over it." She reaches behind me and runs her fingers through the hair on the nape of my neck, pulling at it gently, then stroking the skin beneath, pulling and stroking, pulling and stroking. Gradually the anxiety recedes, as she knew it would, her kind ministrations honed by practice and reprise. My breathing slows. Lucia sighs.

"Let's eat first. I'll make us breakfast. Something hot and nourishing. We need to think what to do next."

"So it's over? They've dumped us? Dumped me?"

"Wait now. Let's eat. There's something I found out but I don't know what it means yet. We'll get there. At least you slept well." The non-sequitur stops me dead as I try to process her observation. I suppose that was her intention, because, as the sounds of whisking eggs and sizzling bacon take over it dawns on me that I did sleep well and that I feel...specifically rested, refreshed even; and that it's morning and I'm having breakfast with my wife. A shimmer of rainbow light quivers delicately against the wall, reflected from a spoon on the table and refracted through a glass of water. The stray sunbeam's component colors resonate with the steady delivery of food and implements as Lucia goes about her business.

It's hard to stay balanced under the circumstances but, yet again, Lucia somehow magically achieves it.

Breakfast arrives accompanied by two more huge mugs of steaming coffee. I think it's time to talk again but Lucia puts a finger to my lips and hands me my cutlery. I don't mind. We eat in what I'm pleased to call a companionable silence. In the end, it's Lucia who speaks.

Lucia

My God, that was a terrible day. I don't know how to tell it. There are lots of people who've said something pithy when in doubt, but I choose Mark Twain to guide me on this occasion. He said, simply, "When in doubt, tell the truth." So here goes.

What could go wrong went wrong and the truth is—in terms of the plan—there's very little to salvage from it all. There's maybe one small thing that might be interesting, or useful, though I don't know how, nor what to do with it yet. There was also some surprising news about Marc's condition, which, now I've recovered my perspective, is heartening.

But already I'm jumping ahead.

Forget Mark Twain. Lucia says, "When in doubt, start at the beginning." Let's try again.

It was a hard start. I hate Marc being fettered by his condition more than I hate the drugs that alleviate it. Though the truth is coming home that I don't suppose I even hate the drugs anymore; in the end, they've become a strange blessing. They're like a narrow rickety bridge over a deep gorge. It might tip us to our doom or deliver us to the other side. So I'll rephrase that, I think: I *used* to hate them, but times have changed. Nevertheless, in this situation we decided that it would be best to eschew them and lend some—how shall I put it—*authenticity* to our visit.

I don't drive so I called a taxi to take us to St. Bartholomew's. As is the way with taxis nowadays the driver didn't know the route. I'm not even sure he'd heard of the place. Instead he put the address into his GPS and drove us straight into the worst of the London rush hour. These people have neither wit nor acumen.

Marc used to drive. He took pride in his cars but he hated, with a passion, driving them through London. He'd curse and rant—albeit mostly to let off steam—and frequently recite his driver's *bête noire:* that driving across London reduces your average speed to six miles per hour. Many of these tropes and conditioned responses remain very much alive in him, even when he's down. So the first hint of the forthcoming mayhem was when, as we jerked to yet another stop, he suddenly lurched at the door. It sprang open and he tumbled out and to the road, upending a cyclist who was unable to stop in time. There were the usual threats and recriminations but I soon put a stop to that. The driver wanted to abandon us but I put a stop to that as well.

Marc had cut his cheek so I held a tissue to his face as we resumed our journey. He'd also torn the knee of his trousers. There was nothing I could do about that. By now we were passing through Stepney and the eastern fringes of the City—my old haunts. I directed the driver along the side roads and we made some better progress for a while. Still, we arrived late. The accumulating delays meant that our appointment was shunted back. Paula was not around to barter with. I could feel the anxiety and tension gathering despite all my efforts to contain it. We sat amidst the sad tide of London's sick, Marc rocking back and forth, uncommunicative, deep within himself. I stroked his neck but I didn't think I was reaching him. Eventually we were called. I helped Marc up, disheveled and detached, and we shuffled after the receptionist, all eyes upon us.

The sick don't judge but their keepers and carers, enraptured by their relative good health, do so with abandon. I heard sniffs and tuts. Someone sniggered. I felt Marc stiffen momentarily but we continued onwards. We were ushered into the consulting room and the door closed behind us, shutting it all away. Professor Gaynes, already standing, swished around his large desk and welcomed us effusively. I noticed his quick eyes move from my arse to my tits, then back again. At least he had the grace to then meet my gaze. His eyes seemed frank and forthright but I thought I noticed something shifty in the set of his hands. They were closed, one tightly, as if holding on to a secret. Still, best foot forward and all that. I put my black voice on, a rich contralto with a touch of accent.

"Professor Gaynes, good morning, and thank you so much for seeing us at such short notice. Paula was very helpful in arranging this meeting."

"Ah, you're welcome. I'm afraid she's off today— I'm not sure why, she didn't call in yet. But anyway, how's Marc? He seems a little, ah, distressed."

"Yes, I'm afraid we had a difficult journey though I'm sure he's calmer now." I could feel Marc relaxing as the small talk continued. I poured on the charm, congratulating the professor on his recent paper to the Association of Neurologists (yes, I follow this stuff) and his preliminary work on the new trial. His eyes flickered at that, but we moved on. We began to discuss Marc's prognosis. He pointed at some scans hanging on the light box on the wall, the finger outstretched, but the fist still closed.

"I don't want to raise any hopes," he began, "but I'm astonished at the atypical morphology of the time series..." He checked himself. "What I mean is that, over time Marc's grey matter—his brain, if you will—could be expected to shrink as the neurons die off..."

I flinched at that.

"I'm sorry Mrs. **Russell,** *Lucia,* I mean. I tend to tell it like it is. Anyway, the point is, they're not, and it isn't."

I got this, I think, but I wanted him to say it again. "I'm sorry—they're not **what?** It isn't what?"

"His neurons aren't dying, as far as I can tell, and his brain mass isn't shrinking. Other elements of the pathological substrate remain, unfortunately. Mainly the beta amyloid plaques, but they seem to be disrupting, rather than destroying, the neurological processes."

This was Marc's theory writ large. I seized my chance.

"Then wouldn't he be a perfect candidate for the trial? A textbook case? A possibility to demonstrate the reversal of the symptoms?" For a moment I was almost breathless with hope, heartbeat, and adrenalin surging at the apparent vindication of Marc's crazy reasoning. I reached for Marc's hand and it grasped mine, as if he was following all this. Then the professor's hand opened and his secret came spilling out.

"The trial's been cancelled."

I felt Marc jerk next to me, as if electrified. My vision seemed to narrow to a thin tube focused on the professor's eyes. Cancelled.

Cancelled?

"What do you mean?" I said evenly, though I wanted to scream it in his face.

"There was a problem. An adverse reaction. Probably an outlier, but we couldn't risk proceeding. Future Pharma Therapies pulled the plug."

Future Pharma Therapies. A part of me squirreled that away, but I couldn't understand what he was saying. I couldn't even speak. Marc began vibrating next to me, a low keening sound in his throat. My silence prompted the professor to fill it.

"To have gone ahead would jeopardize many years of research, not to mention shareholder confidence. The current product will have to be destroyed. It's not quite back to the drawing board but it'll be three years or more before we're ready to go again. Really, I've said too much. I'm sorry."

Will have. To be destroyed. Will have to. Future Pharma Therapies. Shareholder confidence. I tried to determine what any of this meant, but before I could make any sense of it, Marc staggered to his feet, howling.

I was unable to stop him. With unexpected agility, he was up and gone—through the door and away, howling still, his cries now echoing in his wake. Unnerved, I glanced at Professor Gaynes, then scrambled to my feet and ran after him. Already he'd disappeared from sight, though his commotion was like a beacon. I reached a corner and ran headlong into a nurse who was also following the trail of uproar and upheaval. I knocked her to the floor, then ricocheted into some equipment but still kept my feet. Pausing to recover my wits, I realized that the chaotic racket had been replaced by an ominous silence. I looked around, straining my ears. Medics and orderlies were doing the same, heads wagging from side to side as they sought a focus, a clue as to what might happen, or where to go next. There was a squeak behind me. I looked back, startled, to see Professor Gaynes tiptoeing towards me, his rubber soles belying his stealth. He reached down towards the nurse, still stretched prone on the spotless linoleum. I realized I'd stopped breathing. I suddenly realized what Marc meant when he described his life as a series of frozen frames.

Then the alarms went off.

Life went into overdrive.

Those who understood the cryptic signals conveyed by this fresh cacophony began to converge on a broad corridor across the atrium. Galvanized, I made towards it, suddenly aware of the signs and their meaning; RESTRICTED and OPERATING ROOMS and AUTHORISED PERSONNEL ONLY. Careless of these warnings I raced headlong onwards, people shouting and grabbing at me as I fled through the secure area. Then I saw him, held slumped in the grasp of two security guards, blood leaking from his thigh and spotting the pristine floor.

Fear and hopelessness, tinged with what I was appalled to recognize were shame and embarrassment, crowded me with heartrending, gut wrenching, demoralizing pessimism. I felt on the very edge of passing out but realized that wasn't an option. There was still a job to do, if only one of reparation. On cue, Professor Gaynes arrived, urbane and solicitous. I let him put his hand on my shoulder as his eyes flickered around my body again. I couldn't muster any moral high ground to play it wrong and strong, so I plumped for sympathy, casting my flesh into the shape of submissive grief.

"I don't suppose we should continue the consultation," the professor began, as we walked towards Marc. "There's been some damage," he added, quickly qualifying it with "but of course no one's to blame." I nodded, mutely, as he continued. "I can't understand what set him off like that; I can't imagine that he comprehended our conversation. Does he follow your conversations at all? I may have to rerun some of the cognitive tests again!"

If only you knew, you silly man, I thought, too tired and miserable to pick up the thread. Instead, I focused on Marc's bleeding leg.

"Do you think we ought to patch that up?" I asked glibly, directing attention to the damage.

"Of course, of course, I'll see to it myself," the professor exclaimed, which he didn't, exactly, though he did summon a nurse and, together with the burly guards, we shepherded Marc into a small convalescence room and onto crisp, fresh linen. The room was clean, bright and clinical, and I felt a kind of dismal calm take over from the roiling panic that went before. The guards left, and shortly after so did the professor, as effusive on his departure as he was on our arrival. He held my hand tightly as he spoke, as if pressing his secrets into me. I realized dimly that I was richer than before and that some good had come of all this.

The nurse, taking her cue from the professor, was emollient, efficient, and seemingly unperturbed by the morning's calumny. Suffice to say the injury was dressed and Marc was given a tranquilizer, which he surreptitiously spat out. I never did find out where the scalpel came from or how it found its way into Marc's thigh, though I suspect it was an act of self-harm, born of confused desperation. The nurse even chatted a little, matter-of-factly describing Marc's blundering gatecrash into the operating room mid-procedure. Once broached, it was not mentioned again and so I presume no harm was done. Perhaps things like this happen all the time, or perhaps **no one has** any time to deal with them anymore. Anyway, after a little light administration, we were discharged and came home.

No more drama.

Chapter Twelve

Lucia and Marc

Lucia

"So that's it, that's how it went." Marc and I are still sitting at the breakfast table. Empty cups and plates surround us, along with a syringe and two small glass phials, both empty. Marc is using more.

"What do you think?" I ask, but before he has a moment to answer, I'm talking again: "I think it is fantastic news about your head, you know, I mean your brain." I'm uncomfortable, sometimes, being so candid and I recognize how even the smallest euphemisms offer a fig leaf against the hard truth. Then, for instance, "head" seemed something figurative, a healthy, physical, external something – still handsome and unsullied by disease. But "brain" puts the spotlight on the thing inside: the sick thing that's poisoned and dying. Except it is not, I remind myself. And that's what I am trying to articulate, so why the substitute? The answer is that defense becomes a state of mind when you're under siege. "Professor Gaynes said there was no sign of... of... shrinkage. That there should be if, you know..." I trail off. For all my recognition, I'm not good at this.

"It's exactly what you'd expect if I'm right," he replies, sounding bluff, but continues more humbly. "At least, it's what I'd hope." Marc does things the other way round, do you see? He asserts things first, and then qualifies them. We are so different, but we fit. "Anyway, did you look at the scans? What were they like? I kind of missed them," he smiles wryly.

"They looked good. The professor was absolutely right, there's been no deterioration. Just the damned plaques. If only we could get rid of them. It would change things, wouldn't it?"

"I'm certain of it," Marc agrees. "I mean, I have to be. There's not much else to rely on really, is there? But the trial, the fucking trial! And there was me afraid we'd missed it. Now there is no fucking trial. More to the point, there're no fucking drugs. Speaking of which I'm running low." He points to the phials. "But I'll see to that. Tell me what he said again. The prof."

"He said there had been a problem. He called it an adverse reaction, I presumed he meant among the original test people." I concentrated, bringing the professor's words back to mind. I'm good at this, remembering, but prone to embellish my reportage with interpretation. That wouldn't help here. "He said that it was most likely an outlier, an exception, but that they couldn't risk going ahead. Then he said the company had pulled the plug..."

"The company, what were they called?"

"I was just going to say. They were called Future Pharmaceuticals. No, wait, Future Pharma Therapies. They were called Future Pharma Therapies."

"Are you sure? That's two different things you've said."

"Marc, of course I'm sure. I'm just collecting my thoughts. Future Pharma Therapies. Certainly. That's right."

"Then what? You said he told you some more." Marc is looking at me fixedly, with a kind of cold analytical intensity that always makes me nervous, like he's trying to catch me out, but then he relaxes and settles back in his seat. "I'm sorry, I know you'll get it right. I'll shut up."

"He said 'to have gone ahead would jeopardize ten years of research.'" I pause a moment, but I'm much clearer now. "Then he went on to say 'not to mention shareholders' confidence.' Do you want an interpretation?" Marc nods cautiously so I continue: "I'm quite sure that I'm right but I didn't dwell on it at the time, then...well, you know what happened next. Anyway, it's this: I felt he was financially implicated somehow. He looked inwards when he mentioned the shareholders. He was momentarily speaking to himself." I don't want to pollute what little information we have, but having so little, we need to sweat what we've got. No. Now it's said. I'm glad I've aired it so I ask the next question. "That wouldn't be right, would it? There should be some separation between these things, no? To prevent a conflict of interests?" I know Marc trusts me in these things so I don't mind when he just says:

"Go on."

He means it's noted and that we'll come back to it when the picture's complete—which won't take long.

"We're nearly finished. Then he said 'The current product will have to be destroyed. It's not quite back to... I think he said 'square one', no, wait, he said 'we're not quite back to the drawing board but it will be more than three years before we're ready to go again.' Then he said 'Really, I've said too much.' I don't understand that bit at all. Or rather, I don't understand it if he's above board. Anyway, that's it." I stop and there's a brief silence.

"What do you think?" I ask it again, in the proper place this time.

Marc

"God, it's slim pickings, isn't it, Lulu," I reply. She's laid it all out, filling in the—admittedly very many—gaps in my recollection. In exchange for all the mayhem, we've got a name, a suspicion and an inkling that the drugs I so need haven't been trashed yet. It doesn't look much, and yet… and yet…

"Let's find out more about this Future Pharma outfit. I've never heard of them before. They weren't cited as a partner in the Micklethwaite proposal but I'm guessing they're the production facility. As Gaynes explicitly referred to them, I reckon it's got to start there. I'll look them up. Can you do some digging on the prof? His interests and affiliations, that kind of stuff. Maybe his faculty has got a register of interests or something? I don't know, but if you're right, there'll be a needle somewhere in the haystack."

Lucia's looking interested. She loves this kind of stuff. It'd be fun if it wasn't so desperate.

Nagging at the back of my mind is some tiny… absence. Something I haven't recognized or realized. Inwardly I acknowledge that's kind of an occupational hazard nowadays. I can no longer rely on "tip of the tongue" stuff just coming to me when it's ready. But after a second's pause, that's exactly what I do.

Three hours later and I still haven't found any reference to Future Pharma Therapies. I thought I was good at this searching stuff. Even now, my instinct to test tangents and chase down hunches usually pays off. I've tried numerous combinations, permutations, substitutions and alternatives but, no dice. I'm tired, my concentration's waning and my stupid head keeps singing a nonsense rhyme. The words flash through my imaginarium while my teeth click out a stuttering backing track. The rhyme goes like this:

"Better wear your body armor," *boom budda bam,*

"If you're up against that phool phat farmer," *boom budda bam,*

"Cos he ain't nothing" *budda bam*, "but a snake charmer." *Budda bam bam bam.*

Over and again it plays, distracting me further. What the hell's a "phool phat farmer" anyway? I look up "phat" in Wiktionary. It says "African American Vernacular English as a deliberate misspelling of the word fat." I mean, why would you do that?

Then it hits me in the face.

It's *Phuture* Pharma Therapies. This time, amidst Google's many suggestions for alternative spellings, there's one entry that fits the bill; it's an obscure PDF document from something called whittinghaven.com. Here goes nothing. Nervously I click on it and the file opens. I key in a find command. Nestled amidst a huge and unutterably tedious swathe of minor administrative detail is a single meeting note that says: 'Nicholas Mbengwe to establish Phuture PharmaTherapies as an unincorporated entity of Whittinghaven Research Limited.'

Bingo. I think.

Lucia

As ever, I find it so much better to be doing something. Stillness, quiet and contemplation are important to me, but they clot and curdle when I substitute them for action. Or to put it another way, if I resort to pondering when I know I should be acting.

Marc's right, there's not much to go on, but if we must make a silk purse from a sow's ear, so be it.

OK. Professor Gaynes. Let's look him up. Ouch! Not so rare. I add "St. Bartholomew's" to my search.

Aha! Here he is! Professor Charles Aloysius Gaynes to be precise. And he's in Wikipedia. Perfect. Born 1970, prep school, grammar school, gap year in Africa, graduate, master's degree and then PhD in Neurobiology from the University of Cambridge Faculty of Medicine; subsequently research fellow at the University's Department of Clinical Neurosciences, before promotion (I suppose it's promotion) to the department's Director of Neurology. He has a list of publications, articles, and citations as long as your arm, gradually focusing on and specializing in neurodegenerative disorders and finally specific neurodegenerative features of Alzheimer's disease.

His first appearance as professor is at Bart's Hospital, about seven or eight years back, where he led—and still leads—their small neuroscience clinical and teaching unit. He is still a research fellow at Cambridge, though his academic output seems to have declined more recently.

Separately, he's an elected member of the British Association of Neurologists and co-chair of their cognition sub-committee. He's also executive adviser on their neuro-rehabilitation working group and a trustee and board member of the British Alzheimer's Society.

He's single, has no children and, by all accounts, both plays and enjoys Central European chamber music, collects South East African ethnic art and musical instruments and "enjoys walking among our own beautiful woods and vales, especially those amid the lakes of Northumberland."

So, a member of the great and the good: clever, cultured, somewhat posh, and either a loner or lonesome. As far as I can tell. I'm beginning to wonder whether his seeming interest in me is just a figment of my mind, though I'm rarely wrong in these things. Anyway, let's take a look at his registers of interest, though on present showing I can't imagine anything exciting or curious springing out.

Nope. Nothing does. Mostly they just cross-reference one another, underlining and reiterating his elevated but essentially limited position in the world. There are some, admittedly large, research grants but nothing out of the ordinary, certainly nothing that sets bells ringing.

And so I briefly wonder… what *does* he do for sex?

I look over at Marc. He's completely preoccupied, tapping and clicking and muttering to himself, occasionally writing a note or looking into space. I know better than to distract him. He'll appear to ignore me for a while, then smile and say something disjointed or elliptical before re-focusing. Later he'll have forgotten anything that passed between us.

Bored with Professor Charles Aloysius Gaynes, I wonder who or what else might help provide some pieces for our fragmentary jigsaw puzzle. Who, for instance, was the chap who combined Mabetamine and Limenofil? That seems germane. I think back over our investigations, sifting through my recollections: Algernon Benacerrafi. That was him.

Off we go again.

Now, Algernon is altogether more interesting: not famous, nor celebrated, nor particularly gifted at first blush —and there is very little history to calibrate him by. Yet here he is, plucked, it seems, from academic obscurity in northwest Africa after he graduated—albeit with a first— from l'Université d'Alger Département de Pharmacie. He shipped up in Oxford where he worked as a technician at University College before applying to do his master's degree there, specializing in neuropharmacology. During his degree, it seems he came under the wing of one Nicholas Mbengwe, an assistant professor of geriatric pharmacology, who subsequently took him on as his PhD student. It appears to have taken him a long time to achieve his doctorate, though, and there is an unspecified whiff of scandal surrounding his progress. It's not clear what that entailed though there seemed, from the innuendo that collects in the runnels of the gutter press and social media, a hint of sexual shenanigans coupled with a suspicion of—whisper it gently—cheating. There is also the suggestion that he is a sort of high level *savant* and that beyond the slim ray of his intellectual focus, his understanding of the world is naïve and childlike.

Certainly he seems to have come and gone regularly back to his alma mater in Algiers and yet there, as elsewhere, the details remain blurred and the trail stays cold. Nevertheless, he eventually claimed his doctoral degree and went on to become a research fellow at University College.

There are few publications in his name and very little in the way of plaudits generally. What there are suggest he is a drug designer of singular yet narrow talent with a bloodhound's nose for the locks and keys of certain neuro-chemicals and the obscure codes and ciphers of the molecules that affect them.

Then, around fifteen months ago, he visited the University of California San Diego School of Medicine in La Jolla and came back inspired, relatively speaking. A single paper, subjected to a low key but top notch peer review, laid claim to the process by which Mabetamine and Limenofil could be engineered to provide their separate effects in a single compound, each component potentiating the other at the optimum point of therapeutic benefit. Something to do with "oscillating reactions", whatever they are. There was the briefest ripple of interest, mainly in the specialist academic press, then nothing. That's surprising, as the technical hurdles of achieving that are—or maybe, now, *were*—significant. But we don't know. Because nothing came of it except the brief mention of the trial on which we staked our hopes, now aborted.

Why would that be?

It's the formation of *defined* absences within the narrative that make it compelling. Those famous "Known Unknowns" develop a shape, and they can be investigated. From very little—a blank canvas, basically—nodes of information are condensing. And when that begins to happen, soon it will rain.

"Marc, I think I have something that will interest you..."

Marc

"Hang on a second Lulu, I'm nearly there – I'll be with you in five..."

Actually, I might mean ten. I'm on a roll.

From small acorns, mighty oaks do grow! I'm not there yet but the lattice is developing nicely. Whittinghaven Research Limited is a private limited company dealing in mainstream pharmaceutical research, mostly tweaking so-called "reuptake inhibitors" to deliver more precise effects in "older people." According to their website, they have several products in the pipeline and are looking forward to a number of Phase 1 trials. A little more digging and there is a distinct link with whittinghavencare.org, which, through the Whittinghaven Care Foundation, runs a number of geriatric care homes—"for older people with complex needs"— throughout southern and southeast England. I'm not going to begin to speculate on the relationship between a company developing specialized drugs for "older people", especially one moving towards early trials, and a foundation set up to care for said "older people"— particularly those "with complex needs."

But you can.

In any event, the distinct link is Mr. Nicholas Mbengwe, a.k.a. Professor Nicholas Mbengwe, Fellow of the Academy of Medical Science, Research Fellow at University College Oxford, Director of Geriatrics at Oxford University Faculty of Medicine and, get this, Research Center Lead for Geriatric Pharmacology at our own Micklethwaite Foundation at St. Bartholomew's Hospital. Oh, and not to forget where we started, he's also CEO of Whittinghaven Research Limited and Chair of the Trustees of Whittinghaven Care Foundation.

That's some clout. Not to mention vested interest.

I won't run through all of his declarations—which are manifold—but believe me, he's the lynchpin for millions of pounds, dollars and Euros in research grants, gifts, trusts and charities, as well as a range of other vehicles that veer just to the right side of legitimate.

His private life is even more colorful, if that's possible. Born into a powerful Zambian family of impeccable tribal credentials and extensive industrial holdings, he enjoyed the best of pretty well everything his society could offer. He literally raced through school. At sixteen, an alumnus of the ridiculously exclusive Baobab College, he swept the board with armfuls of qualifications, sports awards and a number of citations for his apparently extraordinary grasp of biochemistry. Without pause, he sailed into the prestigious University of Cape Town's Faculty of Health Sciences. His first year was stellar.

Then he came out. Of the closet.

A gay black man, no matter how gifted, privileged, or promising he might be, in South Africa is—by any measure—in for a desperately hard time. Perhaps because of all his success, and the envy that went with it, he came in for much worse. The thing is, it wasn't innocence, purity or even ignorance that brought him down. It was a rare miscalculation born of arrogance, egotism and hubris. How do I know? Because he was a magnet for the media.

Brilliant—probably a rare real-life genius—beautiful, flamboyant, and very rich, he courted celebrity. He encouraged it. He exploited it. He was calculating, controlling, charming and cynically manipulative. He doubtless thought he had them all in his hand. The media sycophantically charted his rise, and then they gleefully documented his fall.

Then he went off-grid.

Two years later he was in London, at Imperial College. There was no messing this time. By twenty-four, he had his PhD. Then he moved up to Oxford and started collecting his many titles.

Chapter Thirteen

Synthesis

Marc

"OK Lulu, let's see what we've got." Despite the marathon slog down so many paths less trodden, and despite the looming proximity of my next inevitable descent, I feel pumped. "How did you do?"

"Probably not as well as you," she smiles. "I noticed you were on a mission. I've been cleaning the house for the last couple of hours – but yes, I've got some stuff." She quickly runs through the information she's gathered about Gaynes. We're both disappointed with the apparent mundanity of his public persona, but I can sense she's got something else, something that's pleased and excited her.

"Well, go on then," I grin, "spit it out. You look like the cat that got the cream."

Even as I say this I'm wondering if she can match my discoveries.

I should gag the miserable fucking impulse that prompts this futile urge to compete. It's ignoble and disloyal and I loathe myself for it. It'll seem all the more pathetic, shortly, when I realize the extent to which this exercise is going to define the meaning and point of teamwork.

"Alright. After the prof, but before the cleaning, I looked up Algernon Benacerrafi." I must be looking blank or something. "You know, the one who combined the two drugs," she prompts. I nod, waiting and expectant, wondering if this will take us anywhere. She runs through her thumbnail biography, which does begin to raise a few interesting questions, it's true, then I hear her saying "...it seems he came under the wing of one Nicholas Mbengwe, an assistant professor..."

"Who?" I demand, roughly, though I know already. "Who did you say?"

"I said Nicholas Mbengwe. Um-beng-way..." her voice drifts out of phase, into the distance. I slump back in my chair. I feel like a two dimensional cut-out, draped, and folded over the contours of the supports beneath me. My poor, strange mind starts to wheel and tick as the tumblers clatter into place.

Mbengwe's orchestrating this. He's chosen arguably the century's greatest health problem and set about curing it. It's his pitch for posterity, his tilt at greatness. His legacy. Kismet or blind chance has put his ambition and my salvation together on the same bus. But, even though we're both strapped in and share the same destination, our progress is relative. For him the bus is on schedule. For me it's running desperately late. He has time—I do not.

He's making his bid for a Nobel Prize while I'm slipping into the dark. The clarity of this formulation calms me. I re-inflate to my usual three dimensions and Lucia telescopes back into view.

"...Marc, Marc, what happened, are you OK? Are you leaving me? Speak. Don't go now, not yet. Wait, please wait."

"No. No Lucia, I'm fine. I'm tired and I'll have to rest soon, well, you know what I mean, but it's alright. You found out something amazing. We found out something amazing. Listen, let me explain." I run through my own findings, illustrating the rise, fall and rise of Nicholas Mbengwe: the glitter, the egotism, the dirt – and then the silence.

"He either reformed..." says Lucia slowly.

"...Or evolved," I finish.

"Quite. People don't so much change as adjust. Some just get smarter and perfect their camouflage."

"So in your world, the bad get worse by getting better at being bad. That's heartening." I'm smiling at her, but she's not amused. Instead she says:

"If you're right, Mbengwe has built a fortress at the heart of the British medical establishment. From there he's ruthlessly organized his assets with the single ambition of beating Alzheimer's. What we don't know is the propriety with which he's done it, but, otherwise—what's the problem?"

I explain my peculiar vision of being on the relativity bus: that we're out of sync, on different sides. Adversaries.

"He's doing what you want. What you need. That's a good thing, right?"

I'm blindsided by her clarity. I was about to launch into a "yeah but, what about right and what about wrong and what about the rest of us" tirade, presumably to bolster my self-defined role as righteous underdog—but I'd be deceiving myself. I mean, of course it's a good thing; and I'll be doing myself no favors trying to hitch myself to some ethical hobby horse, or claim some moral high ground to justify whatever skullduggery might come next—which I was about to. It'd be hypocritical. Worse, it would be stupid. I mean, honestly? Why do I give a shit?

Whatever Mbengwe's ambition and method, I'm just as focused on fixing myself. And just as unscrupulous as to how I achieve it. Lucia has boiled things down to the necessities. Do you remember, back a few chapters, when I asked this:

"How far must we go? (How far will I go? How far can you go?)" and...

"What lines must we cross?"

That's where we've arrived at. The point at which we cross lines and go all the way. Even as I'm registering this Rubicon, I hear Lucia telling me:

"These people aren't our enemies."

"No, but they are obstacles." I reply. Again she adjusts my direction of travel.

"Marc, I'm sorry. You know I'll always support you, but in this you're absolutely wrong. Without this opportunity you'd have nothing." She splays her hands, emphasizing the point. "Nothing at all. Instead, because of it, you have a chance. These people are neither enemies nor obstacles – they're assets. All we have to do is make the most of them." I ponder this for a moment, before acknowledging its absolute truth. She continues.

"That doesn't have to mean we are beholden to them. It doesn't have to mean they have any influence over us. It doesn't even mean we have to acknowledge them. What it does mean is that we must understand their intentions, their vulnerabilities, their exposure and their defenses. Then, whether we approach them or not, whether we make contact or not, we exploit them to the hilt."

Wow. I'm, well, I'm just blown away. Why do I always want to fight? Lucia is just so much better at this. But she's still not through.

"But I think, in the end, we will have to make contact, or think of a way to find out more. There are two significant loose ends, and we need to understand where they fit in. The first is Phuture PharmaTherapies which we assume exists, but about which we know nothing. And the second is Professor Gaynes. He's my big hunch. He's implicated, I'm certain of it. We need some facts."

I ponder this analysis. She's right. Again. I'm thinking how technology might help us. There's virtually no part of modern research—or modern administration for that matter—that doesn't rely on IT.

"We need a hacker," I venture.

"But we don't know any hackers," Lucia points out.

"No, but I also need some drugs."

Chapter Fourteen

Marc

I'm sitting in an extremely smart office just off Harley Street in London's West End. The walls are dove grey. The paint is rich, matte and reassuringly luxurious. The furniture is functional grey leather and steel. Opposite me are four pictures, contemporary abstracts blooming with an eclectic array of potent colors and amorphous shapes that appear to follow no pattern or convention. Perhaps that's the point. The overall effect is sophisticated though ultimately rather anodyne. They're attractive but I don't feel any desire to scrutinize them.

The floor is bleached ash – boards, not laminate. It's wonderfully clean, besmirched by neither smear nor smudge – except for a reddish brown stain just in front of the elegant Regency window. The stain is presently hidden by a granite coffee table. The table is too heavy to move without assistance, and I originally spotted it when an earlier table appeared, between visits, and I thought I'd just, you know, see what was underneath it. The stain must be really difficult to clean.

I'm here to get the drugs I need. I mean the coke and the modafinil. Whether or not there's anything in my bizarre theory one thing's for certain: I'd be as good as dead if I had to get it off the street. Doctor Astrakhan, who I've come to see, is able to provide pure pharmaceutical grade cocaine in the quantities I need to keep me going. The modafinil is easy, of course; it's not illegal and it's readily available.

The coke costs a fortune. More than three times as much as the best street gear. I could probably get the modafinil cheaper elsewhere and be reasonably sure of its provenance but it's much neater to get it all together as well as endlessly reassuring that I'm getting the right stuff.

I'm by myself because Lucia doesn't like this part of my life. I'm also well dosed to avoid any difficulties along the lines of those experienced on the trip to Barts. I actually thought about driving here. I still have a car—a rather beautiful recent model Mercedes, in fact—and by not letting the bureaucratic right hand know what the bureaucratic left hand is doing, I've managed to hang on to my license. I despise driving in London however, where on a bad day the best you can hope for is an average speed little better than a quick walk. So I took a minicab to avoid the stress.

In a few minutes Doctor Astrakhan's astonishing personal assistant will come and beckon me to join him. She's around five feet ten, svelte, alabaster pale with lush raven black hair and Nordic cheekbones you could strop a surgical blade on. She also has a pert round arse—just slightly bigger than you might expect on one so lithe, a not unattractive proposition—and impressive breasts. Amazingly she wears no makeup and appears not to demonstrate a trace of artifice in her immaculate presentation. She'll say, in a peculiar blend of Muscovite and Cockney: "Doctor Astrakhan will be pleased to see you now, awright?" then usher me into his inner sanctum. Her name is Natassja.

To get there, you walk through an apparently ordinary door. Imposing, no doubt, to the casual eye, but frankly amazing if you take a second look. The door is at least twice as thick as you might expect, and thus the door and its jamb are subtly **curved to affect** a precise fit when closed. The door closes against a precision milled flange which completes a surgical-grade hermetic seal. After a few visits, I also noticed the multiple three-inch steel bolts set into the frame, so finely wrought it's almost impossible to spot them in their recesses. I suppose the door itself is also hi-tensile steel, and quite possibly one of two portals let into a similarly structured cage hidden somewhere beneath the elegant dove-grey paint job. I say two because I imagine that, when deployed, the public entrance will become essentially impassable and that it will have been deployed because the occupant needs to exit by another means. One presumably engineered for a swift and discreet getaway.

Such are the requirements of a top of the line doctor come drug dealer.

"Doctor Astrakhan will be pleased to see you now, awright?" announces Natassja, right on cue. I follow her pleasingly round but refined buttocks into the good doctor's consulting room slash fortress. She pauses a moment—I wonder if she's about to curtsey—then leaves, barely touching what must be a half-ton door which, miraculously, hisses shut after her.

Doctor Astrakhan is a youngish looking man with longish brown hair, partially pushed back and several bangs of which have fallen back into place around his slim ascetic face. He has grey eyes set under a deep brow, but a regular seam of humor belies the severity of this arrangement. He's wearing a good shirt with pale red and blue pinstripes, no tie. He looks cool but serious; less doctor, more drug dealer, though his excellent credentials would suggest the opposite. That's assuming, of course, that you were even aware of his principal occupation. He also runs a legitimate practice.

"Marco," (he always calls me Marco, which I rather enjoy) "how are you? Perhaps you've come to discuss cure rather than consumption? Prevention rather than prescription? No? A shame. Really! I'm working hard on a... how might you say... a deviation... no, no, that's not right... a *variation* on aversion therapy. Something I observed while attending some, ah, colleagues', um, advanced negotiation procedures. Very informative. But no, I think perhaps you're after your usual, yes?"

I am indeed after my usual, which has anyway been paid for in advance, but I want something more this visit.

"You're quite right Yakov." Yes – we're on first name terms. We should be, given his fees. "But I wonder if you can help me with something else. I wonder if perhaps you know any IT security consultants."

"Marco...honestly!" He affects a pained expression. "I see that on the simple premise that you know me as a drug dealer you assume that I'm going to have access to any number of other nefarious occupations and their practitioners. Which is, of course, very astute of you. I think what you mean is that you're after someone so familiar with electronic and technological security systems that they're able to assure their impenetrability, or perhaps lack of it?"

"That's precisely what I was trying to say, Yakov. Thank you for expressing it so eloquently."

We tend to banter like this when I'm buying the drugs. It's kind of fun, but I'm glad I'm just a regular client without debts or other obligations. I doubt that would be any fun at all. In any event, as expected, Yakov is my man.

"I think I know the very chap. He's not cheap, but of course you'll know that. He'll charge five thousand Euros per day."

I think I must be registering some shock.

"But don't worry," Yakov continues, emollient, "it's unlikely he'll need more than a day. You pay me." His voice sounded sort of hard when he said that. "Tell me what you want, I'll give you the report. If you can pay today, send me the brief tomorrow— you'll have it within the week. Efficient, yes?"

"Efficient, yes," I smile. I lay out what I want. Everything on Mbengwe. Everything on Phuture PharmaTherapies. And everything on Professor Charles

Aloysius Gaynes. I've brought the notes with me, so I hand them over.

"Excellent, Marco. We're almost finished…"

I transfer two grand there and then, on my phone, promising the rest tomorrow as I'll need to authorize the balance. He's OK with that.

The trust that exists between supply and demand.

Soon I'll leave. Natassja will hand me my drugs on the way out, neatly secured in airtight packaging. I'll lock them in my well-used briefcase and no one will be any the wiser.

It doesn't happen like that.

Chapter Fifteen

Marc

I like Yakov. I kind of relish the not-entirely-vicarious sense of danger he conveys. He's a gangster, no doubt, but he's a clever one and he's got a lot of style.

I really should have gone home after our consultation, but he's managed to persuade me to join him at his members' club, somewhere between Soho and Covent Garden. Natassja's with us too, having first changed into a pair of tailored leather strides and then slung a tough looking biker jacket over her shoulders. She looks more than slightly gorgeous and I'm a little worried that my erection is noticeable as we crawl along in the black cab. I rest my London evening paper across my lap, for modesty's sake. It'll do. I'm not really sure how hard I'm trying.

Behind us, a rich golden sun hangs above the low London skyline and its clogged streets, westering towards Bayswater as the lethargic traffic jolts and jerks through the endless blocked intersections. Aimless crowds of listless people flow around the stuttering vehicles like sacred cows. The cab's meter ticks relentlessly, a handsome return for standing still.

We don't care. Chatting shit, going nowhere.

I'd been about to leave when the first tinge of cold oblivion brushed its dark fingers lightly along the fissures of my brain. I could have made it home, probably. But then Yakov suggested a quick toot and, well, it seemed like the right thing to do, under the circumstances. He'd called Natassja in then lined up three impressive lengths of cocaine on the glass surface of his extensive desk. I don't like snorting it but sometimes you just have to take things as they come. We each leaned forward, banknotes thrust into our respective nostrils and sucked up the lot.

Whoosh. Not bad.

That's when we decided to go out.

Eventually the taxi drops us at the curb and a posh looking doorman ushers us through the lobby and into the cool gloom of a secluded enclosure not far from the bar. Within moments a waiter brings us a bottle of cold, pale Meursault and three crystal glasses. Yakov gestures for me to taste it. It is beautiful. I used to covet white Burgundy of this caliber. The rich butter and honey of the chardonnay grape matured and refined by time and French oak.

It always reminds me of sex.

It's one of my deepest regrets that I can no longer drink it. Or shouldn't, at least. So this is a rare and guilty pleasure, to be cherished and savored. I sniff at it. I breathe it in. I sip at it, then roll it around my tongue, letting it rest a moment. The moment extends. No one seems in a rush. Eventually I nod. Satisfied with my appreciation, the waiter pours out our glasses. He wraps the bottle in a linen cloth, places it carefully in the ice bucket and leaves us. Yakov produces an expensive antique snuff dispenser and hands round three spoons of coke.

"Nice one mate," breathes Natassja, sounding as stoned as I feel, "laaavely drop of Quentin."

Quentin?

She leans forward, grinning deliciously, her tits pressed against the polished mahogany tabletop.

"Quentin Tarantino! Vino! Call yerself a Laaandoner?" She rocks back, laughing and stretching her long legs.

Is she for real? Honestly, Russian and Cockney just don't go together.

I suppose Yakov and Natassja must be lovers. They don't act like it, exactly, but there's an easy connection between them and I wonder quite what we're doing here.

I'm not nervous, exactly, but I'm wondering if I'm in the midst of some spontaneous act of seduction. That would be complicated, even though my treacherous libido clearly doesn't see it like that. Her eyes are fixed on me, glowing.

"So Marco, you want information," Yakov interrupts silkily, breaking the spell.

"What? What information?" I'm nonplussed at his intervention. Pissed off and irritated, though at the same time reluctantly relieved. "Oh, you mean the hacker. Yes. It's a little, um, industrial espionage. Can't really say any more."

"Oh, now, Marco—I think you can! What do you say, Natassja?"

"Industrial espionage." She laughs again, head cocked; white, perfect teeth. "He is a shpion. A spy! An English collar and tie. Mate."

"It's funny," Yakov continues, more or less ignoring her. "I recognized their names. Mbengwe and Gaynes. Big in neuroscience. Drug delivery. Specialist stuff. I'm surprised you didn't mention their, ahem, colleague. You know. Algernon. Algernon Benacerrafi."

I sober up instantly, libido going into reverse. I can't imagine but that it shows. My sobriety, obviously. What does he know? More importantly, how does he know it?

"Come on, Yakov, you must know I'm not going to talk about this stuff. I've paid for the hacker— I would've thought it ended there."

He looks at me for a long time.

"Quite right too," he eventually agrees. "But I wouldn't have thought this was your... natural element."

"Nor yours," I counter, unusually blunt. "What's your connection?" I don't suppose he'll answer me. It doesn't matter; I just want to shift the focus elsewhere. But unexpectedly, he does.

"Hmmm. How shall I put this? I have an interest in neurological continuity. There are times when some of my... patients need sustaining beyond their normal capacities. So I follow some of their work. Algernon in particular has some interesting ideas. But I'm wondering now how you—Marco— and I intersect so closely, all of a sudden?"

He pauses again and clasps his hands. He makes a steeple of his forefingers and rests his chin on his thumbs. The steeple is pressed to his lips as if he's stopping any more words from coming out. I feel nervous. I'm sweating. Probably the coke. Or fear. Then he lowers his hands and breathes out.

"Perhaps it's coincidence, yes? A few lines of coke and our brains are too slippery. Perhaps one more and we'll be over the hill. Natassja, what do you say? Another? One for our spy? Or one for the road?"

"I think our shpion has lost his mojo," she says, looking at me full on, eyes now gleaming with a different kind of light. There's no trace of Cockney any more, just pure Muscovite. "I think, Yakov, you and me should go back to the office and fuck. Marco must go home now."

It's been a tiring day.

So that's what I do.

Chapter Sixteen

The Inhibitionist

Stil rwong, the uvver
man is. Me, uvver me.
Clevr me.See? Not rwong
wrong but not finnisht.
Aksing for infomayshn
on computes not enouf.
Need kno how peepl
work.
Tel you this: Mbengwe
from past. He, the
uvver udder od other
man, other me Kno him
but can not rmember
him, Go bak far an he
there.
Think hard now. Write
right. Send good
message.
Here.

Marc. You must call Donna Fulbright & ask her about Gaynes and Mbengwe. We know them from old.
Tuk v. lung to doo that. Fnde an copi ever wrd. Tired now,
go.

Chapter 17

Report

Lucia

The neurologists talk about something called plasticity. In their world, it means the capacity of the brain to reorganize itself following changes within the body or in the external environment. In the normal brain, plasticity—more specifically neuroplasticity—is implicated in the process of learning and adaptation. It's particularly strong during childhood when new experience and information requires rapid adjustment. Neurons, the brain's special cells, the pathways of our thoughts and actions, join and separate as our lifetimes' experiences shape them. If we're damaged, physically or psychologically, the healing process will often involve forging new pathways. It's like a roadblock that impedes us. If we give up, we stop right there, unable to progress. But some extra thinking, some extra work, usually means we can work out an alternative route and continue our journey.

There are around one hundred billion neurons in the brain. That's as many stars as there are in the Milky Way. Every one of those neurons can connect to another ten thousand neurons. In a healthy brain, there are maybe one thousand trillion connections.

Plenty of ways around **the roadblock.**

I think Marc is making full use of this plasticity, aided by his unconventional regimen. Which, as he would have it, is also protecting him from further damage. As this appalling story continues, as the roadblocks mount up, as the obstacles multiply—both internal and external—he just keeps going around them. Finding new routes, new solutions. Refusing to give in. I hope that when we get to the end of it, he's prepared to make his own contribution to the solution. He has a unique story to tell. I believe he will, as long as it's on his terms.

But I digress, though not entirely.

We have the report. We've cleared another roadblock.

Report://x-mal 23_05_2019
Stop.
hydra 192.154.1.70 https-form-post
"/w3af/bruteforce/form_login/dataReceptor.php:user=^USER^&
pass=^PASS^:Bad login" -L users.txt -P pass.txt -t 10 -w 30 -o
hydra-https-post-attack.txt
Scriptprogress
Hydra v11.2 (c) 2019 x-mal
Hydra (http://www.thc.org/thc-hydra) starting at 2019-05-23 13:11:03
[DATA] x tasks, x servers, xxx login tries (l:x/p:x), ~x tries per task
[DATA] attacking service https-post-form on port 80
[STATUS] attack finished for 192.154.1.70
[80][www-form] host: 192.168.1.69 login: **Baobab1baby** password: **mGluR5>0** 1 of 1 target successfully completed, 1 password found
Hydra (http://www.thc.org/thc-hydra) finished at 2019-05-23 16:21:07
Forward selected data.

1.
\\Panther\scansnet\.Trash-1000\files\ALZ_DMZ\PPT\premarket

Phuture PharmaTherapies:

Unconditional belief. Absolute Determination.

Problem Statement

"Neurological disorders are among the world's greatest unresolved health problems, and Alzheimer's disease is one of the biggest threats facing modern post-industrial societies. *There is currently no prospect of a cure for Alzheimer's, only the possibility of slowing its progression.*"

Phuture PharmaTherapies categorically rejects this. On the contrary, the prospect is now within our grasp.

Flush and Fortification

Introducing the Harmonized Oscillatory Resonance Reaction. No fancy acronyms. Just genius science and sublime innovation that brings us to the cusp of a medical revolution.

Take a mixture. Each component works, in isolation. Combine them, for convenience. Then leave their delivery to chance and their separate actions to fate. Satisfied?

No, of course not.

By contrast we have licensed and refined the world's only two drugs with proven capacities to dispel amyloid and promote neuron regeneration. Our unique formulation has been nano-engineered from first principles to deliver the complex compound across the blood brain barrier. But that's child's play compared with our next maneuver: *in vivo*, the component structures resonate together, each potentiating the optimum therapeutic effect of the other before handing over the baton. This provides an elegant pincer movement which dispels the amyloid, normalizes the neurotrophic signaling and ultimately reboots the neuronal synapse.

Some will call it a paradigm shift. We call it Flush and Fortification.

<u>Responsible action means risk management</u>

Research entails responsibility. It also involves risk. That's why we will always balance the highest ethical standards with finely tuned risk modeling. Our approach assures regulatory approval *in situ* including pre-clinical laboratory studies as well as rigorous clinical trials.

Our pre-publication paper and all associated data form part of this prospectus and are available only as part of our general and particular non-disclosure conditions.

Bids to capitalize the Phuture PharmaTherapies' Flush and Fortification program will begin at 11.00 GMT on 01/06/2017. Secure details can be obtained at http://14.160.34.106/ using your Panther participant username and password. These further details, if obtained, form part of this prospectus and are available only as part of our general and particular non-disclosure conditions.

2.
\\Panther\scansnet\.Trash-1000\files\ALZ_DMZ\PPT\funding
SECURE Memo
To: Unity 1, Nairobi
Date: 12/06/2017

Greetings Waheshimiwa,
I am most glad to hear we have an agreement. You have our account details and we look forward to your deposit in due course.

Control.

3.
\\Panther\scansnet\.Trash-1000\files\ALZ_DMZ\PPT\funding
SECURE Memo
To: Unity 2, Mumbai
Date: 26/06/2017

Most Excellent Sirs,
I am most glad to hear we have an agreement. You have our account details and we look forward to your deposit in due course.

Control.

4.
\\Panther\scansnet\.Trash-1000\files\ALZ_DMZ\PPT\funding
SECURE Memo
To: Unity 3, Paris
Date: 08/07/2017

Mes bons amis,
Il a été un pleaseure faire des affaires avec vous. Vous avez notre details du compte et nous nous réjouissons de votre dépôt en temps opportun. Nous allons bientôt discuter des installations avec vos collègues estimés.

Control.

5.

\\Panther\scansnet\.Trash-1000\files\ALZ_DMZ\PPT\funding
SECURE Memo
To: Control
Date: 14/08/2017

Hi,
Attracted but need more collateral. Face to face helpful,
primary researcher much preferred. Can do?

Unity 4, La Jolla.

6.
\\Panther\scansnet\.Trash-1000\files\ALZ_DMZ\PPT\funding
SECURE Memo
To: Unity 4, La Jolla.
Date: 02/09/2017

Hi,
Asset incoming. Ready for debrief.

Control.

7.
\\Panther\scansnet\.Trash-1000\files\ALZ_DMZ\PPT\funding
SECURE Memo
To: Control.
Date: 03/10/2017

Asset in place. Looking good. We have your details and
agree the terms.

Unity 4, La Jolla.

"Now I think we know who the shareholders are," I remark drily, looking over at Marc. I'm pretty sure we're on the same page. "Those people are in the shit. Every which way."

"They sure are," he murmurs, flicking to the next page. "I'm thinking back to what you said. Mbengwe's doing a good thing in a bad way and now it's grinding to a halt. Let's see what happens next…"

8.
\\Panther\scansnet\.Trash-1000\files\ALZ_DMZ\PPT\peer-review
SECURE Memo
To: Pawn.
Date: 05/11/2017

You're back. Good. I hope you behaved yourself. You know I'll find out. Anyway, it's time to publish. I think we can be assured of an excellent panel. Submit tomorrow.

Control.

9.
\\Panther\scansnet\.Trash-1000\files\ALZ_DMZ\PPT\commission

07/11/2017, 18:43
To: Micklethwaite Board (Group1)
From: Nicholas Mbengwe, Geriatric Pharmacology (Lead Member)
Subject: Alpha-Mabetamine/Limenofil-X7 Oscillating Reactor Composite Phase 1 Trial
Attachment(s): Modelling#1_#5.zip

***

Colleagues,

I have some good news. Algernon has submitted his paper for review.

As you know, I have been monitoring his work closely and I'm absolutely certain that this is pure gold. The computer models (attached) surpassed the most stringent safety requirements during processing by all general algorithms as well as the relevant classes of contextually specific variants. In-vitro testing has produced spectacular results measured against even the highest expectations.

I think it would be prudent to begin the process of commissioning Phase 1.

I realize this might seem rather precipitous, but once the paper is published the principle is out there and the market will be snapping at our heels. I see this as a once in a lifetime opportunity to put the Micklethwaite Foundation on the map, up there with the Wellcome Trust and the other big guns.

Of course, I recognize the need for propriety and hence I suggest that I take on a purely administrative role. (I could also begin to put out some feelers on the finance front if you wish. I think you'll agree I've had some success with that in the past!)

That being the case, I would venture to suggest that our colleague Professor Charles Gaynes might be the ideal candidate to lead the project. He's admirably qualified and he's one of our own. If the Board wishes I can make initial overtures?

I look forward to your views.

Sincerely,

Nicholas

10.
\\Panther\scansnet\.Trash-1000\files\ALZ_DMZ\PPT\commission

22/11/2017 10:07
To: Nicholas Mbengwe
From: Dominic Allsop (Chair)
Re: Alpha-Mabetamine/Limenofil-X7 Oscillating Reactor
Composite Phase 1 Trial

***

My Dear Nicholas,

I'm sorry to have taken a while to get back. The Board only met yesterday. To cut a long story short we welcome your proposal and applaud your acumen.
We broke your proposal into four motions.

1)   That the Micklethwaite Foundation commissions the trial as sponsor
2)   That you adopt the administrative role
3)   That Charles be appointed project director
4)   That you begin raising funds

I'm pleased to say that all motions were passed unanimously. You may proceed. The Board will expect a project mandate early in the new year, then quarterly reports including progress against targets, deltas and, of course, accounts.
As you know the Micklethwaite is going through a lean time just now so I'm afraid this is all going to be rather light touch.
Best of luck. We have every confidence in you.

Dominic

11.
\\Panther\scansnet\.Trash-1000\files\ALZ_DMZ\PPT\commission

24/11/2017 17:41
To: C.A. Gaynes
From: Nicholas Mbengwe
Re: Alpha-Mabetamine/Limenofil-X7 Oscillating Reactor
Composite Phase 1 Trial

***

Charles,
See below.
As expected the Board signed off on my little idea. We're on!
I'll contact you later using the secure system.
Bye for now,
Nick
...

12.
\\Panther\scansnet\.Trash-1000\files\ALZ_DMZ\PPT\commission
SECURE Memo
To: Foreman.
Date: 24/11/2017

I'll be routing finance through a Whittinghaven unincorporated subsidiary called Phuture PharmaTherapies. It's all set up with accounts, constitution, registered office, the works. You're sole trustee. Congratulations! You're a powerful man! And don't worry, I'll look after the pennies ☺
Pawn's paper is on its way but we don't have to wait until the review's complete before getting started. Accordingly I've booked us both on a flight to Niš Airport. They call it Constantine the Great Airport! Nine flights per week! Oh, the high life.
Never mind, we're routed via Berlin (much nicer) and I've arranged a little stopover for the night. We can have some fun! Just like old times.
Anyway, put the 9-11th December in your schedule. On the 10th we're going to see a man about a lab, on the 11th we're going to see the Regional Director of Health Services regarding the trial authorization.
Ciao!
Control.

13.

\\Panther\scansnet\.Trash-1000\files\ALZ_DMZ\PPT\commission
SECURE Memo
To: Control.
Date: 27/11/2017

Sorry Nick, I was at a conference, didn't see the emails. Berlin sounds marvelous.
If you're right about the trial, this could be the breakthrough we need. I'm not sure I understand the admin stuff, and "unincorporated" sounds rather informal for so much money! Perhaps we could look at the papers. During the trip?
Look forward to it. I miss you.

Charles

14.
\\Panther\scansnet\.Trash-1000\files\ALZ_DMZ\PPT\commission
SECURE Memo
To: Foreman.
Date: 28/11/2017

DON'T use personal identifiers again, fool. And don't bother me with "papers."

Control.

15.
\\Panther\scansnet\.Trash-1000\files\ALZ_DMZ\PPT\commission
SECURE Memo
To: Control.
Date: 28/11/2017

I'm sorry. Don't be angry. I'm not really used to this.
Foreman.

16.

\\Panther\scansnet\.Trash-1000\files\ALZ_DMZ\PPT\commission
SECURE Memo
To: Control.
Date: 12/12/2017

We did it!
Loved Berlin. You're sooooo....
I'm in. All the way. Didn't you say that to me???

Foreman.

17.
\\Panther\scansnet\.Trash-1000\files\ALZ_DMZ\PPT\commission
SECURE Memo
To: Foreman.
Date: 12/12/2017

Naughty. Don't flirt.
But yes, we're on the way. It'll be hard work. Stand by.

Control.

18.
\\Panther\scansnet\.Trash-1000\files\ALZ_DMZ\PPT\commission
SECURE Memo
To: Control.
Date: 14/01/2018

Are facilities underway? We're $50m into this. Progress required, backers anxious. We've also heard some unpleasant rumors.

Unity 4, La Jolla.

19.
\\Panther\scansnet\.Trash-1000\files\ALZ_DMZ\PPT\commission
SECURE Memo

To: Unity 4, La Jolla.
Date: 14/01/2018

Stay calm! No details please! Partners will recall that we await publication pending peer review.
Which is imminent.
I think you'll find the rumors are just that.

Control.

20.
\\Panther\scansnet\.Trash-1000\files\ALZ_DMZ\PPT\commission
SECURE Memo
To: Foreman. URGENT
Date: 15/01/2018

U.S. concerned. Need urgent confirmation from Europe.
Lab status?

Control.

21.
\\Panther\scansnet\.Trash-1000\files\ALZ_DMZ\PPT\commission
SECURE Memo
To: Control.
Date: 19/01/2018

Confirmation unforthcoming.
Status as expected. Awaiting publication.

Foreman.

22.
\\Panther\scansnet\.Trash-1000\files\ALZ_DMZ\PPT\commission
SECURE Memo

To: Foreman.
Date: 19/01/2018

Damn. We need the paper.

Control.

23.
\\Panther\scansnet\.Trash-1000\files\ALZ_DMZ\PPT\peer-review
SECURE Memo
To: Broadcast.
Date: 03/02/2018

**Peer review complete. Overwhelming support.
Preparing to seek approvals.**

Control.

24.
\\Panther\scansnet\.Trash-1000\files\ALZ_DMZ\PPT\peer-review

Press Release.
BioMedia: London. 04/02/2018.

Cautious welcome for Alzheimer's development.

A recent paper from Oxford Research Fellow Doctor Algernon Benacerrafi, working on behalf of a private international consortium, describes an innovative formulation of two leading Alzheimer's therapies. The therapies have been demonstrated as effective in mice, as well as a wide range of virtual models.
Defective amyloid protein was reduced and neuronal function restored over a period of six weeks.
Algernon Benacerrafi said; "This is a significant advance on preceding therapies. The mice showed substantial improvement across the entire spectrum of cognitive functions. We look forward to further in vivo studies."
Ends.

Note to Editors: For further information about the Alpha-Mabetamine/Limenofil-X7 Oscillating Reactor Composite contact BioMedia at info@biomedia.com/AML

25.
\\Panther\scansnet\.Trash-1000\files\ALZ_DMZ\PPT\peer-review
SECURE Memo
To: Foreman.
Date: 10/02/2018

Perfect! With press like that who'll give a shit! Let's keep it no-profile.

Control.

26.
\\Panther\scansnet\.Trash-1000\files\ALZ_DMZ\PPT\commission
SECURE Memo
To: Control.
Date: 06/03/2018

Confirmation! Phew. The paper clinched it. Without raising a scintilla of interest. Payments expedited, all local permissions obtained.
Seeking jurisdictional approvals.
Final funds incoming via ~~REDACTED~~ **S.A.R.L. Internal transfers to follow. We're set.**

Foreman.

Chapter Seventeen

Breakdown

27.

\\Panther\scansnet\.Trash-1000\files\ALZ_DMZ\PPT\build
SECURE Memo
To: Control.
Date: 14/03/2018

Report attached. Encryption key via DKN protocol#1-alpha.

Foreman.

28.

\\Panther\scansnet\.Trash-1000\files\ALZ_DMZ\PPT\build
Decrypt successful/
Phuture PharmaTherapies Laboratory and Testing Facilities
Progress Report to 12/03/2018

Accommodation (Green)

Interim progress as per specification.

Analysis/Lab (Green)

- Magnetic Resonance Imaging (MRI) scanner (Magneton Ultra 7T system): on order.
- Positron emission tomography–computed tomography (Biograph TruePoint PET/CT): on order.
- Integrated analysis and diagnostics (Syngo PET Amyloid): on order.
- Molecular Diagnostics (VERSANT kPCR): Installed, tested, online.

- Immunoassay Systems (ADVIA Centaur XP Immunoassay System Assays): on order.
- Electrophoresis and Proteomic assays: sourcing in progress

Compute (Green)

- Servers (local 16 stack PowerEdge R930 Rack Server RAID array).
- PCs.
- Network (bespoke Cisco secure network).
- Dedicated fiber optic connection to MEDComp private cloud facility.
- Local array on order.
- Network specification in progress. Fiber optic connection uncertain in locality. Contingencies are limited to local private circuit (copper) or dedicated satellite link.

Hey, this is Niš.

Human Resources (Green)

- Profiles established. Agencies consulted. Target: All staff in post by 25/01/2019 (One year).

Test subjects (Green)

- First tier trawl ready. Awaiting Clinical Trial Authorization (local jurisdiction).

Meds (Green)

- Twelve beds with full life-sign monitoring and analysis, and intensive care support systems. Specification in progress.

Supplies and logistics (Green)

- Specifications in progress

<u>Spend</u> (Green)

- Optimal to date. Accountancy report to follow end-month.

Confirm all strands green. Gantt performance optimal.

Report ends.

29.
\\Panther\scansnet\.Trash-1000\files\ALZ_DMZ\PPT\build
SECURE Memo
To: Unity 4, La Jolla.
Date: 15/03/2018

Good news. All green. Report forwarded for your consideration. Encryption key via DKN protocol#1-alpha.
Sorry for the delay but I think you'll agree it was worth it.

Control.

30.
\\Panther\scansnet\.Trash-1000\files\ALZ_DMZ\PPT\build
SECURE Memo
To: Control.
Date: 18/03/2018

Sighs of relief. Backers content. Will await updates as available.

Unity 4, La Jolla.

31.

\\Panther\scansnet\.Trash-1000\files\ALZ_DMZ\PPT\build
SECURE Memo
To: Broadcast.
Date: 13/05/2018

Approvals granted. Regulatory hurdles cleared

Control.

32.
\\Panther\scansnet\.Trash-1000\files\ALZ_DMZ\PPT\build
SECURE Memo
To: Broadcast.
Date: 28/08/2018

Project on track. Limbering up for commencement. Report attached. Encryption key via DKN protocol#1-alpha.

Control.

33.
\\Panther\scansnet\.Trash-1000\files\ALZ_DMZ\PPT\build
Decrypt successful/
Phuture PharmaTherapies Laboratory and Testing Facilities
Progress Report to 28/08/2018

Accommodation (Green)

Complete as per specification.

Analysis/Lab (Green)

- Magnetic Resonance Imaging (MRI) scanner (Magneton Ultra 7T system): Installed, tested, online.

- Positron emission tomography–computed tomography (Biograph TruePoint PET/CT): Installed, tested, online.
- Integrated analysis and diagnostics (Syngo PET Amyloid): Installed, tested, online.
- Molecular Diagnostics (VERSANT kPCR): Installed, tested, online.
- Immunoassay Systems (ADVIA Centaur XP Immunoassay System Assays): Installed, tested, online.
- Electrophoresis and Proteomic assays (leased from BioMedCorp): Installed, testing in process.

Compute (Green)

- Servers (local 16 stack PowerEdge R930 Rack Server RAID array).
- PCs (various, hi-spec machines as selected by staff, to be hardened by SecCorp GmbH).
- Network (bespoke Cisco secure network).
- Dedicated private circuit to MEDComp private cloud facility. Hey, we tried. Checks out at 100Mb/s
- Local array and local machines installed and tested. Connectivity confirmed. Ramping throughput.

Human Resources (Green)

- Salaries agreed and confirmed, references confirmed, contracting complete. Termination clauses itemized. Nondisclosure clauses notarized.
- All staff in post by 25/01/2019.

Test subjects (Green)

- Second tier sift complete. Third tier (bio-profiling) underway on one hundred individuals, using in-house facilities cross referenced against three control facilities. Target fourth tier population fifty for Phase 1 pool selection.

<u>Meds</u> (Green)

- Twelve beds with full life-sign monitoring and analysis, and intensive care support systems. Installed, tested, online.

<u>Supplies and logistics</u> (Green)

- Contracted, incoming on schedule, pipeline secure.

<u>Spend</u> (Green)

- Optimal to date. Accountancy report to follow end-month.

Confirm all strands green. Gantt performance optimal.

Report ends.

34.
\\Panther\scansnet\.Trash-1000\files\ALZ_DMZ\PPT\build
SECURE Memo
To: Broadcast.
Date: 28/01/2019

Project commencing. We're good to go.
Abridged report attached. Encryption key via DKN protocol#1-alpha.

Control.

35.
\\Panther\scansnet\.Trash-1000\files\ALZ_DMZ\PPT\build
Decrypt successful/

Phuture PharmaTherapies Laboratory and Testing Facilities Progress Report to 28/01/2019

<u>Analysis/Lab</u> (Green)

- Electrophoresis and Proteomic assays (leased from BioMedCorp): Installed, tested, online.

<u>Compute</u> (Green)

- All machines tested and online.
- Dedicated private circuit to MEDComp private cloud facility tested and online.

<u>Human Resources</u> (Green)

- All staff in post.

<u>Test subjects</u> (Green)

- Fourth tier population ready for Phase 1 pool selection.

<u>Spend</u> (Green)

- Optimal to date. Accountancy report to follow end-month.

Confirm all strands green. Gantt performance optimal.

Report ends.

36.
\\Panther\scansnet\.Trash-1000\files\ALZ_DMZ\PPT\intermission
SECURE Memo
To: Control. CRASH URGENT
Date: 04/04/2019

Fourth tier test individual severely unwell, following unscheduled Phase 0 trial (first-in-man). Indications of cytokine release syndrome, including angioedema and major organ dysfunction.
I've administered corticosteroids and implemented plasma-exchange procedure. I don't think it's working. Oh God oh God.
Three other subjects, unharmed, showing signs of amyloid disruption and dispersal. Monitoring carefully.
Facility under lockdown.

We shouldn't have done this. It was too soon. Oh God, his head. Oh God

Foreman.

37.
\\Panther\scansnet\.Trash-
1000\files\ALZ_DMZ\PPT\intermission/crypt
SECURE Memo using Cisco one-time encrypt policy
To: Foreman. CRASH URGENT
Date: 04/04/2019

You shouldn't have sent this. Lockdown = silent protocol. Stop sniveling and treat your *private* patient. Full cordon. You understand.
I want all data on well subjects. Repeat all data.

Control.

38.

\\Panther\scansnet\.Trash-
1000\files\ALZ_DMZ\PPT\intermission/crypt
SECURE Memo using Cisco one-time encrypt policy
To: Control.
Date: 06/04/2019

**Silent protocol intact. Unwell subject deceased, body
repatriated expeditiously.**
**Other subjects unharmed but unbetter. Amyloid
deposits ARE flushed but cognition unimproved.
Fortification failure. Neurons dead as dodos.**
**The trial's over before it's begun. What next? We've
spunked getting on for $100m. We're fucked.**
**Data files enclosed. Encryption key via DKN
protocol#1-alpha.**

Foreman.

39.

\\Panther\scansnet\.Trash-1000\files\ALZ_DMZ\PPT\intermission
SECURE Memo
To: Control.
Date: 15/04/2019

**Hi, Unity 1 looking for a progress update.
Anybody there? LOL**

Unity 1, La Jolla.

40.

\\Panther\scansnet\.Trash-1000\files\ALZ_DMZ\PPT\intermission

SECURE Memo

To: Control.

Date: 20/04/2019

This is Unity 1. Anybody there? Where the fuck are you? Seriously now. Update imperative.

Unity 1, La Jolla.

Chapter Eighteen

Lucia and Marc

Lucia

So there it is.

Isn't it curious how corruption can be so easily reduced to process? So glibly rendered as procedure. Isn't it breathtaking how events so scandalous can be described in terms so technical, in such dry bureaucratic jargon? I suppose the answers are inherent in the questions, and they are: no, it is not especially curious, and no, it is not particularly breathtaking. In the end, these are just tactics— tactics used over and again, down the ages—to make something iniquitous appear mundane. Most importantly, these tactics are used to couch the unacceptable in terms that make it tolerable to those involved even though they are aware, no doubt just below the surface of their actions, how entirely immoral their actions are.

We all do it. We call it "pragmatism."

What did Marc say to me, playing back my own words? "Mbengwe's doing a good thing in a bad way." I didn't care then and I don't care now because, more importantly, he hit the nail on the head when he added that it's now grinding to a halt. That is worse, much worse, for us. In the end, what price scruples when our only tangible lifeline is about to be severed.

The report also puts our task into a frightening and almost overwhelming context. Our plans and devices seem tiny against the weight and scope of this venal endeavor. I ponder a moment longer. I need to tread carefully.

"What do you think?" I ask Marc.

"'Flush and Fortification' eh? I think they stole my catchphrase. I also think we've come a long, long way in a short time. Barely two weeks ago we were panicking about me not being accepted for a drug trial. Minor bribery was the worst of our thinking. Now, if we cut to the chase, we're about to... blackmail, I suppose you'd call it, a criminal organization led by one of the country's leading medical scientists. I remember asking you how far we'd have to go and what lines we'd have to cross. Well, I think we know now."

I consider his words. He's right, in a way. But he's still looking at the situation through his inevitable filter, seeing it as adversarial, as a confrontation. He's either forgotten his recent admiration for my diplomacy or feels we've gone beyond it. Perhaps he thinks he's been reasonable, done the right thing, and that now it's time to take the gloves off.

I'm afraid the same will go for Mbengwe and his team. Knowing men, especially men backed up against the wall, I'm afraid their instincts won't be constructive. They'll see it as a fight. They'll escalate. Their pride will precede their fall, even though the fall will be precipitous. We can't let that happen.

A germ of an idea flitters through my head, then crystallizes.

It's a game changer, a gamble, and I don't think I can tell it just yet. Not to Marc. It is this: The distance we must travel, and the boundary we must cross is that *we must join with them*. I described these people as assets and assets they are. It seems to me they need recovering. I take a deep breath. This will be difficult. "We'll go as far as we must but we need more information if it's to be on our terms. What else do we know about...?"

I'm cut off.

"What else do we need to know?" he grinds out, hard and cold. "The hacker report says it all. They're in the shit, up to their necks. I don't know how they hope to get out of it but if we make our move before everything blows up we've got the advantage. We've got some real leverage. I'm scared thinking how little time it's going to last."

"Marc, we can do better, but to do so I need to know how they work. Otherwise we're just going to get caught up in their bullshit. Imagine we confront Mbengwe. Will he run? Or will he fight? Would he try to burn Gaynes? Or Benacerrafi? Or both? Or no one at all. We just don't know. We don't know their dynamic. Or maybe we go after Gaynes. Then what? Is he loyal? Would he break? He's in love with Mbengwe, or something similar. Would he take the fall? And Benacerrafi. He's strange, he has a peculiar mind. Would he even understand the problem?

"What I'm saying is this: we've got one chance to get it right. So we've got to get it right. We need to know more before we make our move."

"Lucia, I think we're wasting time. You're right on one thing. We've got one chance, so let's get on with it. Personally, I'd go for Mbengwe. He's got the biggest stake in it. He's got the most to lose."

"So let me get this straight," I'm beginning to feel a flush rise through me. "We let Mbengwe know we know he's fucked, as if he doesn't know already, then tell him what? That we'll stay quiet if he gives you his drugs? Do you think you'll feature in his contingencies, given the scale of this? You'll just be another thing he's got to shut down, or run away from. Marc, it's a recipe for disaster. We've got to do better than that."

"So what's your plan? Eh? What've you got?" Marc sounds both defiant and shaken. For all his talents, I suddenly realize he's not up to this. He's a fighter—as in he won't give up but he's not a warrior. He hasn't got the moves. Not when it comes to this.

"Look, Marc, I know how to do this." I speak slowly, reassuringly, and I hope I sound more certain than I feel, but, now we've contemplated the crude, blunt edge of blackmail, and the ensuing chaos, I'm sure my way will be better. "What I need is for you to take more of your drugs and think how we can get the other side of the story. OK? Will you do that? This time tomorrow, if we can't come up with something better, we'll push the button, we'll go nuclear. But for now I need to find out what makes them tick."

"Why?" he asks, sullen and resentful.

"Because. Because I don't want to threaten them. Because I want to work with them. I want to help them so they can help you. Because to help them I need to know how they work. You're part of it.

"Will you do it?"

Marc sighs, looks at me askance, then shrugs and grins. "Yakov's latest gear is particularly engaging. I'll get straight onto it. No problem."

Marc

I don't really understand what Lucia's up to. On the other hand, I've seen how she operates enough times to trust her. We used to work in Government, before all this. Both of us were quite senior, dealing with the big guns and their political advisers. I did well because I was analytical, and if I was also critical it was because that's where the analysis took me. Though I often won, I also sometimes lost and I was getting to feel a little bit like a square peg in a round hole. Even if I'd remained functional, I don't imagine I would have got much further. I'm not sure I would have cared.

Lucia was going places. Her big asset, her gift, is her emotional intelligence. Her empathy. Unlike me, she consistently prevailed (though she'd no doubt reject that word as combative); she prevailed by building consensus. She would get her way.

Damn! "Prevailed." "Get her way."

You see? My entire vocabulary—my world view—is based on competition. I can't help it. The sad thing is I'm not even very good at it.

Instead, she sees the best possible path down which everyone gets a piece of what they want. She says things like "let's see if we can find some common ground" and "here's how we can move forward together" and the thing is, that's what happens.

In my world, facts are facts and you use them like levers to get what you want. In her world, facts are relative and the important thing is to get the right perspective. I've thought about this a lot and, in the end, statistically, her way works better than mine.

In other words—I'm not clear what she's doing, but I'm confident she'll get it right.

Chapter Nineteen

Marc and the Inhibitionist

I've taken the drugs and my mind's ticking like a bomb. Obviously, while this dark therapy works, overdoing it is never a particularly good idea. The fall is worse. The damage mounts up. While my Alzheimer's might be kept at bay, I'm sure some other part of me is suffering. Unfortunately we're here at the end game. Whatever Lucia has got planned, if it doesn't work, it's over. I'm over. Sure, I'll keep this up, but it's not going to fix me. I'm aware that I don't even know if Mbengwe's stuff will, but there's nothing else. Nothing even close.

What I'd really like is... well, just to go on. That's what we all want really, isn't it? To go on. We're not well equipped to deal with the opposite: to stop going on. To stop.

So I'll keep it up. Visiting Yakov, keeping strange hours, following drug trial notices, fucking Lucia, watching TV, going to the shops, buying food, making food, eating food. Washing, bathing, studying myself in the mirror. Does the internal decline show? Can I clean it off?

On and on, round and round. All of it on a false premise unless Lucia puts things straight.

And in between all of these things, visiting with *him*. The other one, The Inhibitionist, who is myself, the other *me* on the other *side*. I haven't feared him, so far. He's a shadow and little of his experience makes it through the chinks in our transitions. At times, he feels more like "rest", or "sleep", though I know that isn't all he is. What about all that stuff he writes to me? I've collected reams of it. Some of it reads like a rather stupid child's diary, recording trivial events, laboriously and badly. Occasionally something he says shines a ray of light on my experience, or experience more generally. It's made me wonder, at times, when I've not been focused on getting better, whether, as the lights gradually go out, those that are still on shine brighter by comparison. Many of his recollections I—I mean me, as of now—can't bring to mind, and those I can lack the clarity of his version of events. Other times he puts things together about me—I still mean this me, now—that I didn't, or couldn't see. Those things, when I read them, illuminate my present tense.

Having said all that, I've been too busy to really look at his scribblings of late. I've seen some, lying around, mostly on my desk or by my computer.

He knows where I live.

But I've not read them and for now I don't suppose I will, because I've got to crack on and help Lucia with her stuff. Where to start? How the hell am I supposed to find out how these people co-exist? Work together? Play together? Fuck together by all accounts. I don't know. Gossip columns? Private Eye? The *Lancet?* I haven't got a fucking clue. Where's my laptop? I'd best get started.

Oh bloody hell. He's slipped one inside, one of his little notes. Ok, Ok, let's take a look.

Jesus, I didn't realize I went out on midnight rambles. People driving me home like some lost animal. How does that happen? Has Lucia got me some dog tags or something? I'm pretty sure I don't have any idea of the way home when I'm in that state. Then there're all those little flashes of humor. Sex even. Jesus. And what's all this about biotechnology? Badly spelt mostly. Biotechnology! Wow, I used to do that a long time ago... wait.

What's this?

What the fuck? What the fuck is this. Look. Look at what he's saying. He's saying something. I'll read it:

```
"Marc. You must call
Donna Fulbright & ask
her about Gaynes and
Mbengwe. We know them
from old."
```

Just what the fuck. It's like ectoplasm or something, like a voice from the other side. A message. I can feel the hairs standing up on my back and neck. Fuck.

I need to look into this. Wait. Let me check this stuff.

Oh man. He's been trying to reach me. He's been saying it for ages. Him. The Inhibitionist.

Me.

I've—he's been processing the relics of our memory, way down there in the dark; burrowing patiently through our past, working it out, transferring it from deep forgotten pathways that are all but lost to me. And I've been ignoring him. Perhaps to my cost, because I think he's on to something. I think what he's saying is what Lucia wants.

```
"Aksing for infomayshn
on computes not enouf.
Need kno how peepl
work. Mbengwe from
past. Kno him. Go bak
far an he there."
```

"Computes." He means the hacker, I'll bet. He means that his report is only half the story. That the other half is about the people in it. We need to know how those people work together. It's almost precisely what Lucia said.

Good God. He says I know Mbengwe already! Then there are these urgent little passages reminding me about this woman called Donna Fulbright, someone I'm supposed to know. The trouble is I don't. Look:

```
"Meny yeres a go werked
in govornament. In
siense sience.
"Caled BIOTECHNOLOGY.
Wuman hoo grate frend.
Donna Fulbright.
Importnt. Big wuman
```

like boss sHe kno
sientests.
"Spechally abotw
ALZHEIMRS."

***

"Go to docters sune.
Lusha wil make vem do
ritghte But not
byvemselvs. Must
rmember boitecnogology
wuman"

***

Marc. You must call
Donna Fulbright & ask
her about Gaynes and
Mbengwe. We know them
from old."

***

Wow. Just wow. He must really have worked on that last
one, struggling to make it clear and correct. For me! I

suppose it was his best shot so—if I'm to give any credence to this, which I am—I think I'm going to do exactly what he tells me. I'll tell you why. It's because he also said this:

```
"Funy thing is remembr
far back wen slo. Can
be good becorse all gon
uther times."
```

He—or maybe I should say we—*we* remember things differently and we remember different things. I think he means we've got to work together.

```
"Think this"
```

I think this too.

Chapter Twenty

Marc

Donna Fulbright. Dame Doctor Donna Fulbright no less. Prompted by my darkling shadow I've looked her up. Between the internet, some old papers and correspondence and a bit of hard thinking, I've more or less grasped the essence of her, even recovered some recollections of when we worked together. Now all I need are her contact details. A telephone number would be ideal.

Donna Fulbright was the head of a dedicated division of government responsible, during the heady days of the new millennium, for the promotion and exploitation of biotechnology. The administration at the time had prioritized certain elements of scientific research and development, believing—with some justification—that Great Britain could lead the way in their growth and commercialization. The minister responsible was a Peer and a billionaire.

Donna was his right-hand woman.

Medical and pharmaceutical industrialists, entrepreneurs, university vice-chancellors and heads of faculty, as well as quacks, dreamers and chancers, all lined up for her patronage. Of course, government doesn't call it patronage nowadays but the licenses, grants, legislative advantage and strategic influence that flow from such relationships are little different, in practice, from days gone by. Nevertheless, Donna was noted as a tough nut; hard, straight and fair. Thus the queue was longer, the blandishments more effusive and the stakes much higher than with her predecessors. She, in turn, was blithely candid, sometimes combative, and sometimes caustic—

unless she wanted something, whereupon her charm was radiant.

I joined her during this happy hey-day, a rising functionary with a flair for technology and communication. I was different from the civil servants that surrounded her, perhaps a little less fawning, perhaps a little more dashing than she was used to. Anyway, we became friends and eventually I became her confidante. The minister would demand her advice, she would demand mine—eventually the minister just came straight to me, on certain issues, for which Donna was grateful. She had an extensive brief and a lot on her plate.

Eventually I moved on but we remained friends, dining occasionally at one of the clubs that certain echelons of government were wont to frequent. We talked openly about most things, I would tease her a little and at times she would gently remind me of my place—usually with a laugh, never unkindly. I learned a lot from her—though not enough, I'm afraid, to ensure that I became properly senior material after I left her employ.

We lost touch before I got ill and, as is the way with Alzheimer's, memories that aren't used quickly blur and slip away.

But I think I've got enough to sound like I'm just catching up, after a long absence. I don't want her to know the truth, nor what I'm after. I've written some notes and some prompts. Hopefully I can get her to do most of the talking. From what I recall that shouldn't be too hard. I've found her number. It's ringing. Here we go.

"Hello, Fulbright speaking."

Fulbright. I suppose that's some halfway house between Donna and Damehood. It's not where I would have wanted to start, but still.

"Donna, it's been a long time. How the devil are you?" There's a slight pause as she ponders who might be the source of this question.

"Well, damn me. You've either developed a bad case of nostalgia or an urgent need for something. I'm presently inclined to the latter. But to answer your question, I'm largely buggered and I don't mean in a good way. I've got MS, I can barely walk and I'm as fat as a pig, but for all that I'm in fine fettle. So was I right?"

There's no point in treading around things. She's as blunt and acute as ever and though it's terrible news about her health, she won't be at all forgiving of pity, even if it's sincere. Perhaps later, if it seems appropriate. I kind of sigh, wrapping up a number of feelings.

"Yes, of course you're right. I'm not really the nostalgic type." I suddenly change my mind about revealing my own illness. I won't tell her everything but perhaps it will help. It's partly because of her own revelation and my instinctive urge to make a connection, and partly because it will make this conversation easier and probably more productive. "I'm having some trouble with my memory. I'm sort of buggered too." I pause, but she just waits. "I'm going back a long time. I wonder if you can remind me about Nicholas Mbengwe, his work, his associates, anything that..." She cuts me off.

"What do you mean, a long time? That's recent history unless you've had your head in a hole." She stops, perhaps reflecting on her words. "Then again you sound as if you do have your head in a hole. Or a hole in the head." Well, don't give, don't get. I wouldn't have expected sympathy—except of the roughest sort—even if I'd thought about it. That was probably it. "So? What do you want to know?"

This has become difficult. I've no idea what her reference to "recent history" means, but it certainly sounds as though I should find out. I suppose I'd better hedge.

"Well, I was particularly interested in his relations with two people, Professor Charles Gaynes and Algernon Benacerrafi, and whether they were involved in the, ummm, recent business." It sounds lame.

"Oh Marc, they're what the recent business was about. You're not very good at this, are you? Or else you're worse off than you make out." It sounds like a question. It's my turn to remain silent.

"OK, it would help if you'd confide in me, but let's go the long way round. You'd better take some notes if you're that forgetful."

"Donna, you know..." I want to tell her it's complicated, but she continues over me.

"So Marc, are you sitting comfortably? Then I'll begin. It starts with a young Charles Aloysius Gaynes, an impressionable fellow, callow and somewhat sheltered, who ships up in Zimbabwe for his gap year—something that was, in those days, very much the preserve of the privileged. He's a little confused about his sexuality, back then, but not for long. He travels down to South Africa where he meets a young black man, a veritable cock of the walk, gifted, talented, rich and deeply exotic to our teenage middle Englander. On top of the sights, sounds and new emotions he's experiencing, he finds out that he's being adopted by this paragon and that, to cap it all, said paragon is a talented scientist, probably a genius and certainly way beyond anything that our young fellow hopes for or conceives of for himself.

"Then he realizes just how much he's attracted to his new idol. His dark skin, his lean, strong physique. Within days, he's seduced, hook line and sinker. They become lovers.

''How do I know all this? There's the rub. I was there, you see. Charity work for Médecins Sans Frontières. I've never really confided this—at first because I was faintly scandalized by my own actions and then, later on, because, well, it might have been taken wrongly. I had them both. I used to watch. A proper little ménage.

"We were thick as thieves, the three of us. Sexually tangled, intellectually driven and ideologically bound to the idea that science would deliver the world! We made a pact to see it through. 'All for one and one for all', we'd say, delirious with potential.

"It was marvelous. If only it had been true.

"We were Nicholas's patsies. His pawns from the start. It didn't feel that way at first but, gradually, it became obvious. We moved from being confederates to his willing tools. He explained how we would be his advocates, his acolytes, his apostles, primed to overcome the many prejudices against him and to pave his way to the gilded halls of academia, here in the heart of the old empire!

"He really felt that way, you know. Despite his wealth, intelligence and status, he was a textbook product of colonialism—still rife, then, in southeast Africa. It was one of wellsprings of his ambition to transcend the 'yoke they've laid across my black back.' Of course, Charles and I worshipped that black back, sweating and heaving as he pleasured us both in the bewitching African heat.

"It was around then, as these lines were being drawn, that we first met Algernon Benacerrafi. Nicholas introduced us. He was a beautiful, slim Arab— eyes like dark wells of promise that drew you into his presence. He had fine-boned patrician features and thick lush ringlets that cascaded around his perfect face.

"He looked like a messiah.

"He had a singular mind, able to memorize and process millions of molecular structures and interactions, like one of today's most sophisticated computers. But there was something wrong. He couldn't relate to us, or to anybody, properly. He just watched us as we used his delicious flesh. Nicholas was the worst. I'm afraid something dreadful possessed him when we... played together. It wasn't good. I'm not proud of what we did.

"Eventually we came back, to London, to real life. For a while the energy and promise of our adventure propelled us forward. Charles and I were still entranced by Nicholas, regularly sating ourselves in bouts of abandoned sensuality. We flaunted our relationship, imagining ourselves as radical sophisticates. Defiant, determined, and driven, we dedicated ourselves to our careers, confident in our ambition.

"Charles was always more smitten than I, though, and—as our little pact gradually took on more and more reality—I began to put some ground between us. More and more of Nicholas's ruthless nature became apparent—to me at least—and as our respective careers developed and flourished, I realized that the positions we held and those we would go on to were vulnerable to accusations of corruption, given our circumstances. I'm afraid I slid back on occasion. Lust and idealism don't easily relinquish their grip.

"Even during the period that you worked for me I did some questionable things, for him, things that if exposed would have compromised me, perhaps even led to my downfall – and of course that's exactly what Nicholas threatened to do when I continued to cool towards him. He threatened me with exposure, with mutual disaster. 'All for one and one for all,' he'd say, cynically, when I bridled.

"So Marc, are you keeping up? Is this what you want? I'm not asking why you want it, now, am I?"

No Donna, you aren't. Is it useful? I've no idea. Suffice to say, I wasn't expecting this. Certainly it's remarkable material, illuminating our conclusions with unexpected and unimagined detail. Does it help? I've no idea. I'm recording it on my iPhone, so that Lucia can work out if it provides us with any leverage that might makes a difference.

"It's...helpful Donna. An amazing story. A little overwhelming to be honest, given where you've all ended up. I think I see why you drifted apart, over time. So what suddenly made this 'recent history'? That's what you said, right? All this 'history' suddenly became 'recent.' What happened? Tell me." For a moment, I think she's going to withdraw from the confessional. Perhaps I've been too demanding. The silence extends, then extends further. Then she speaks again.

"Nicholas became increasingly dominant. I suppose Charles and I enjoyed pretending to be his playthings, to an extent, but it was a game. We observed boundaries. But Algernon... Algernon brought out the beast in him. They formed an awful symbiosis thriving on power and punishment. It was sickening and compelling in equal measure. Somewhere down the line we all became implicated. As I said, it wasn't good.

"Nicholas fostered his dependency, consciously and ruthlessly. He controlled Algernon. He kept him on a tight leash, sometimes literally. For all this, he is Nicholas's weak spot, I think. Not in a gentle way, rather his perfect manifestation of subjugation—something he will never willingly relinquish, something he will protect even in the face of reason.

"Nevertheless, he also remained astutely aware that Algernon was an unusual and singularly useful prodigy. To be fully functional, he needed to be educated so Nicholas paid his way through university—a fairly obscure establishment in Algiers, where Algernon came from. It must have been difficult, by which I mean it must have taken a lot of time and money, being there and greasing faculty palms. Nicholas used to come and go regularly, when we were in South Africa, and when we came back.

Eventually Algernon got his degree, a first, which was probably critical to the next phase.

"Nicholas brought him to Oxford—he'd moved up there by then, already an assistant professor. He took Algernon on as a PhD student. They were indiscrete, visiting private clubs that turned out to be anything but. Rumors were rife about their behavior, and then came the allegations that Algernon's work was being ghosted. There's no doubt that Algernon's is an extraordinary talent, but his wider capacities are, well, limited. I'm afraid Nicholas's oversight went beyond propriety. I was quite far removed by then, but still he called on me to help damp down the fires. I helped cover it up. It was my last favor, but not their last indiscretion.

"A while back, a little less then eighteen months I'd say, the three of them—Nicholas, Charles and Algernon—went to California. They were mostly in La Jolla, to negotiate a licensing deal for some innovative medicines. They also went up to San Francisco—a group of them, including their hosts. I gather they were quite active on the gay scene there— and the murkier edges of it in particular. There were allegations, of drugs, assault and blackmail. A toxic combination which soured a promising endeavor, I was led to understand at the time. A possible therapy for... oh my goodness!

"Oh Marc. That's what you're after. You think he can help you with... with your Alzheimer's. Don't you. You think he can help you with your hole. The hole in your head! Tell me I'm right. How do you know? What have you found out?"

So much for prudence. I might as well have told her straight out. I need to wrap this up. I improvise.

"I've been doing some research. It's sort of difficult, now, but I can still think, and as long as I keep notes, well, I get by. I needed to know more about Mbengwe and his work, and a little bit about Gaynes and

Benacerrafi. I don't know how it'll pan out though. But yes, I'm trying to help myself. Is there anything else you can tell me?"

"I don't think you're being quite open, are you Marc? There's more to this than meets the eye. Never mind. It's all water down the drain now and I'm not sure if I care. If what I've said is helpful, well and good. The truth is, I'm not sure what happened next. I only heard about any of it through back-channels, and then only because the diplomats and Consulate people wanted some background. Another cover-up, probably, a fig-leaf for the dignity of the Establishment and the preservation of gross domestic product. I'll tell you this though, he won't survive another. It'll be three strikes and out for the lot of 'em."

"What about Gaynes?" I ask. I just need to get to the end of this. Her realization of what I'm after seems to have upset her.

"He's still Nicholas's bum-chum I suppose. In love, probably. Eternally willing and endlessly useful. All the things I stopped being. Now look at them and look at me. They've formed quite the little cabal there at the center of things. Me, I'm fucked and finished. Where's the fucking justice in that? Tell me!"

I'm embarrassed to hear her like this. I have to go. I remember I'd considered offering her my sympathy. It doesn't seem such a good idea now.

"There is no justice, Donna. There never was. We have to play the cards we're dealt. You know that. Look I'll tell you if this goes anywhere, I'll keep in..."

"Oh, just fuck off, Marc." She puts down the phone. I feel numb, like when something that was once treasured comes abruptly to an end.

Oh well. I got what I wanted.

Chapter Twenty-One

Marc and Lucia

Marc

"Pure gold," Lucia exclaims excitedly. "This is fantastic. And the key was locked up in your head!" She thinks about this for a moment, then says, "Well, you know what I mean." She hugs me, for all the world as if we're free from the weight of my affliction. I'm touched and lifted by her confidence.

I know what she means though. The other one, the Inhibitionist, has brought us to the information we needed to finally spin together all the strands of our peculiar story. We know who and how, and the where and the why. What I don't know is…

"What are we going to do with it?"

Her jubilant expression turns suddenly serious, but her face loses none of its animation, nor her eyes any of their sparkle. She's not long since finished an intense scrutiny of all the information we've gathered, flicking back and forth between our files, notes and the recording of my conversation with Donna, presumably correlating the detail and chronology of the narrative. I'm exhausted, too tired to even think about it. I'm not going to take anything else now. Drugs, I mean. I'll coast a little— it's been a job well done— then relapse. Tomorrow's another day.

"I can see you're exhausted so I'll keep it simple. They've got form, Mbengwe and company. Plenty of scandals and skeletons in the closet, now with the biggest of them all ready to burst it open. They're comprehensively finished—humiliated, disgraced, discredited, vilified, broke and soon to be prosecuted, probably. In short—utterly ruined. And they know it. Unless…" Lucia pauses, perhaps for dramatic effect. "I'm going to give them one last roll of the dice." She wags her finger towards me, emphasizing her words. "Do you want to guess what it is?"

"I can't," I reply because I have no idea.

"I'm going to give them you!"

"Me?" I say, stupidly. It's fair to say I don't know what she's talking about.

"Now we've got the full picture, there's only one thing going to save them.

"You. Think about it. They treat you. It works. You're the first person cured of Alzheimer's. Ever. You'll be better. Everything else will go away. It's the perfect resolution. If it fails, well… look, you've staked everything on this strategy, you believe in it, you've made me believe in it. It's not going to fail. We won't let it, they won't let it. You're as much their get out clause as they are yours."

I really am very tired now, but, I have to say, my wife is brilliant. Brilliant. Though I can barely remember why.

"You're brilliant. Amazing. There's…" I'm beginning to slip away. What was I going to say? "There's a chance…"

"…a chans…it culd work."

Lucia

He's gone. To sleep, mercifully, perchance to dream. I wonder if he does dream, and if so, of what? Well, I'm going to have to leave that for another day because times a-wasting. It's been percolating, this idea, for a while. The folly of threats and coercion. The opportunity cost of the struggle. The clarity of our mutual interest.

Right now they're sitting on a ledge, on a thin crease in the sheer wall of a dark, deep chasm, legs dangling, waiting for the long drop. Over yonder, on the other side, there's the golden light of a brilliant tomorrow, now quickly fading as the future withdraws its promise. Perhaps they'll look down, into the abyss, and with the febrile hope of the doomed imagine that the thickening darkness will soon become dense enough to offer them purchase, like the clouds you see from an airplane window. That they can still clamber towards their shattered dreams, while knowing the impossibility of that hope.

If they accept my proposition, if Algernon's drug works, if Marc gets better, the results will be earth-shattering. At a stroke, they can both reverse their fortunes and turn the world on its axis. Instead of being paraded by the press as base criminals and sordid pederasts, instead of having their bizarre games pored over in gleeful, prurient cinematic detail, and instead of becoming the soon-to-be endlessly molested *bitches* that is their certain destiny once ensconced at Her Majesty's Pleasure, they can become the super heroes of modern science, saviors of the generations to come, giants, world beaters, and superstars.

So now I'm going to offer them fairy wings. I'm going to help them cross the chasm. I'm going to phone Paula, Professor Gaynes' secretary. I hope I can catch her before she leaves for the day, because I don't think we have much time.

"Oh, hello again Paula, it's Lucia—Mrs. Russell… yes, yes, I know, twice in two weeks, we'll be moving in soon! I'm awfully sorry to be calling so late. I wondered if I could have a word with Professor Gaynes, it's rather urgent? Oh, that's a shame. Do you know when he will be in? No? Ok, could you give him a message, I think he'll be interested and it's quite important. Yes. Yes, here it is. It's probably best to get it exact otherwise he might not understand, it's referring to some other people we've been consulting. It's just this: 'Mr. Foreman is no longer in control at the Panther Institute, but that he has the belief and determination to see it through.' Shall I repeat that? No… good, that's right. I know it's a bit cryptic but it's something we spoke about, you know, when we were last there. Before the shenanigans.

"Great, yes, please, do that. You've got my number, haven't you? That's right. Oh and I think we'll be coming by in another couple of months? For a check-up? OK, I'll wait for the details. Do try and get the message to the professor, won't you? OK, I won't keep you. 'Bye for now, have a nice evening, 'bye."

Well. She said she'd email it to all of his accounts and text it too. She really is most obliging. I must buy her a little present. Anyway, I hope it isn't too cryptic. It shouldn't be. It features his codename, Mbengwe's code name, their project's encrypted file header and the key words of Phuture PharmaTherapies' pompous little slogan. If he misses that lot, it'll be because he's already packing his bags. Assuming he isn't, I should get a call later on or tomorrow. I hope so because, right now, I don't know what else to do. I suppose I could try to get in touch with Mbengwe but, to be frank, I'm rather frightened of starting down that route. He's a daunting proposition, dangerous maybe, but mainly I'm afraid he won't see the sense of things as readily as the professor. No. I'm not going down that route. Besides, the more I think about it the more I reckon I'd be doing it because, for once, I'm afraid of waiting.

This is going to be tough.

When I was a schoolgirl, I learned how to wait. The key was never to rush, to play the long game. It was just like my father said: "Everything comes to those that wait." One of my biggest challenges came from Rosie Hamlet, a brittle, egotistical girl with neither charm nor wit. Nevertheless, her boastful arrogance and wealthy background garnered her popularity in some circles. Unfortunately, those circles intersected with mine. I failed to kowtow to her preening, self-referential behavior and refused to be sucked dry by the vacuum that was her character. So she made me her enemy. An early victory against me was her manufacture of a situation which got me expelled from our home economics class, in those days effectively equivalent to a course in cooking and cleaning. This was problematic at first, but I quickly realized its providence by taking up real economics instead.

During a year in which I learned of Keynes and Capital, I also kept a keen eye on Miss Rosie. She was fixing to flunk, and how. I heard she was looking to cheat her way through it and that word had got to her teacher. I took great pains to obtain an advance copy of the Home Economics matriculation paper. I slipped it into Rosie's satchel, left a note on her teacher's desk and, for good measure, anonymously told the school district that cheating was rife and where they would find the necessary evidence.

They made an example of her. I passed my course and I took her down. It cost me time and took patience but it was worth the wait.

Bitch was staying in the kitchen.

He calls at 2:37am. I'm on the sofa in our study – in the midst of a fitful sleep, dreaming about catacombs and corridors that never come to an end. Fortunately I come to quickly and completely, my mind sharp and prepared. The incoming number is prefixed with 381. Serbia. I've got my notes ready and I activate the phone's integrated recording device. Then I take the call.

"Hello, Lucia Russell speaking." I'm not going to say any more. I want him to start.

"Ah, Mrs. Russell. Good. Good." He makes some preparatory noises, throat-clearing and other dysfluencies, and I feel a spark of optimism light up. He's no good at this, and he hasn't prepared. "I got a message from Paula." Still I remain quiet, waiting. "She said it was urgent." Good. I'd said it was important. I'd said nothing about it being urgent. My first contribution will be to set him straight, to put him on the back foot.

"Professor Gaynes, how good of you to call. Though it is rather late." He seems about to start apologizing but I continue. "Actually I said it was important, and that I thought you'd find it interesting." Again I lapse into silence while he ums and ahs. Just as he's about to speak again, I interject. "Perhaps it was you who thought it was urgent?" Now it is he that goes quiet, but I wait him out.

"What do you know?" he finally asks. I smile. The stray thought crosses my mind that he probably can't dance very well either. Then he puts himself out of the game. "What do you want?"

Bingo.

"I want to help you. I think you might need some help. Wouldn't you say?"

"How can *you* help? Who are you people anyway? How do you know so much? We never meant for this to happen you know. We only meant to do good." Good Lord, he's panicking already. I'm glad, but I need to move quickly to steady him. I put on my sweetest, darkest voice, all throat and dulcet rhythms. I'll be his nurse bringing comfort, his priest offering salvation, his lover providing relief. Then I'm going to be the cavalry coming over the hill.

God, I should have been an actress.

"Professor, my dear man, we're not 'you people' at all. We're just Marc and I, struggling to make the best of things. Having said that, we do have some resources, which have helped us get to the bottom of what's been happening. But most importantly I'm offering you the means to not only make your problems all go away, but to realize—no, to better—all of the goals for which you have strived."

"How can *you* do that?" He sounds bitter and contemptuous. I rein in a maverick thought that he deserves the torrent of shit that is heading towards him. It's not constructive. "Everything's already coming apart, Nicholas will be here tomorrow and then..." He stops, I imagine because, this time, he's caught himself saying too much. "What do you know anyway? You're bluffing. You know nothing. I'm putting the phone down..."

Fortunately I've planned for this. I read him probably the most personally wrenching section of the hacker's report.

"Wait just one moment, Charles—may I call you Charles?—I think you should probably hear this. It's from your encrypted communications channel. Your words, I think. Listen:

'Fourth tier test individual severely unwell, following unscheduled Phase 0 trial (first-in-man). Indications of cytokine release syndrome, including angioedema and major organ dysfunction. I've administered corticosteroids and implemented plasma-exchange procedure. I don't think it's working. Oh God oh God.'

"You said that on..." I pretend to consult my notes, but I know it by heart, "the fourth of April, this year. Would you like me to continue?" I imagine him slumped, ashen-faced, considering the extent of our knowledge. It's time to get back to positives.

"I said I wanted to help you, Charles. I do. Listen carefully. You'd agree, I think, that my husband Marc appears to be at the wrong end of middle stage Alzheimer's. Indeed, you diagnosed his position on that miserable continuum. Now I'm going to play you a short segment of a recording he made today. He was speaking to an old friend of yours, Donna Fulbright. You'll hear her first. Please do listen carefully."

I press play on Marc's iPhone and hold it close to the mouthpiece. Donna's voice rings out, clear and authoritative.

"Oh Marc. That's what you're after. You think he can help you with... with your Alzheimer's. Don't you. You think he can help you with your hole. The hole in your head! Tell me I'm right. How do you know? What have you found out?"

"I've been doing some research. It's sort of difficult, now, but I can still think, and as long as I keep notes, well, I get by. I needed to know more about Mbengwe and his work, and a little bit about Gaynes and

Benacerrafi. I don't know how it'll pan out though. But yes, I'm trying to help myself. Is there anything else you can tell me?"

I stop the playback.

"Amazing cognition, wouldn't you say, all things considered? That was Marc, this afternoon. Now, if I were to wake him, he'd be just like when you've examined him. Typical middle to late stage Alzheimer's. Poor cognition, very little awareness, minimum communication and extreme apathy. Marc believes that Algernon's new compound, your 'Flush and Fortification' approach, can save him. If it can, then you'll have vindicated yourselves. You will have reversed Alzheimer's disease. I'm sure your contacts can minimize the several inconveniences—for inconveniences they would become, measured against the magnitude of your success—that have accrued.

"Now, Charles, what do you say?"

"I... I'm struggling to understand this. I'd guess you were attempting some sort of extravagant confidence trick, but that would suggest you were mad, frankly, to put so much resource into something so... so... pointless and twisted. If I assume you aren't mad, and that this is not some complex fabrication, and then suspend all of my scientific credulity for a moment, well, I might ask, hasn't your husband already cured himself? And, that being the case, what's in it for us?"

"Good, Charles, you're back on form. I'm not denying there's a bigger story to tell here, but you can be the ones to tell it. Marc will make himself entirely available to you, on our terms; all he requires is that after you have established the baseline of his, ah, wider circumstances, you administer the therapy."

"Look, Mrs. Russell, before I can agree to anything I'm going to have to discuss this with..."

"Charles. None of us have the time to discuss things. Each of us will end up precisely where our present trajectories dictate unless we act. Those are not good places, for any of us. I believe you're in your laboratory in Niš, yes? There's a flight tomorrow, via Berlin. Perhaps Nicholas is on it? We also have tickets. We can all talk about it in person. You can examine Marc at your leisure. Will you meet us?"

"I... I'm not sure. I don't know what Nicholas will say. He may..."

"Charles. Please. Think. You will all be traduced if you don't find a way out of this. The world will not be a big enough place to hide. Marc and I will do nothing to accelerate that, I promise, but the clock is already ticking. Surely you realize that. And Marc will die of his illness. Those are our present trajectories. Our alternatives are life and success. Think about it. We'll meet you at Constantine the Great Airport at 3pm, or soon thereafter. I've enjoyed our conversation and I think we can look forward to happier times. Good night, and God bless."

I put the phone down.

They'll be waiting for us. I'm sure of it.

Chapter Twenty-Two

Marc and Lucia

Marc

I'm not sure what I expected of this, my first visit to Eastern Europe. Desolate and broken factories, perhaps, relics of forgotten endeavor, now long past producing anything of use. Stark monoliths left as testaments to a brutal and bygone Soviet era. Rows and columns of faceless concrete apartment buildings. There is indeed a little of all this, but it's fascinating rather than oppressive—and once you take it into account it turns out that Niš is a rather beautiful town. Punctuated by abundant greenery and studded with architectural surprises, the city center is neatly and elegantly distributed along both banks of the Nišava River—a gentle tributary which flows ultimately, via the Southern and Great Morava Rivers, into the Danube just east of Belgrade.

At a little under 450 miles northeast of Istanbul, Niš might narrowly justify an historic claim to be at the frontier between East and West, though Sofia—capital of Bulgaria and 100 miles closer—may well take issue with that. Still, it's been around since 279 BC so it can lay claim to its fair share of historical gravitas, not least being the birthplace of the Roman Emperor Constantine, founder of Constantinople and the first Christian Emperor of Rome. He went so far as to craft, with his predecessor Licinius, the Edict of Milan which effectively legitimized Christianity throughout Europe.

At the end of the Second World War, Niš was the only place where U.S. and Soviet forces have ever engaged one another, in a confused and destructive "accident" involving sustained friendly fire. Some historians cite this as contributing to the cold war that followed when what was then Yugoslavia, and Niš within it, became a communist satellite of Soviet Russia.

But enough of history. Let's fast forward to the future.

Nowadays, Niš claims to have a vibrant industrial economy, citing a number of enterprises professing to have thrived following their emancipation from the limitations of communist rule.

But it doesn't, and they haven't.

Some were destroyed in the shameful cluster bombing of the city by NATO forces back in 1999. Others have been bought by multinationals and either systematically stripped of their assets or have simply failed to deliver. Small wonder, then, that as the twenty-first century's teenage years draw to a close, it has one of the highest corruption ratings in Europe, notably in healthcare. Unemployment is high. Wages are low. Against all the odds, this is offset by low crime rates, low perceptions of criminal activity and an overall high perception of the quality of life.

In short, as long as you've got the money and the contacts, it's a great place to do business. Transparency need not be a chore, regulation need not be a barrier, and neither ethical nor moral constraints need be a problem.

I guess that's why I'm here.

Here, this moment, is Constantine the Great International Airport, Gateway to Niš. As Lucia predicted, it's a little after 3pm. The day began very early and I had to fix up quickly. Since then we've been four hours in the air and three hours in Berlin Schönefeld airport, a rather dreary facility a long way south of the city. There's been no sign of Mbengwe, which I see as ominous though Lucia insists it isn't.

We're in a small queue waiting for passport control. I've got two well wrapped grams of cocaine stuffed up my arse and another four clenched lightly between my buttocks. Fortunately this does nothing to detract from our carefully cultivated appearance as a handsome, well-dressed couple eager to sample the opportunities afforded by this vibrant, go-ahead city.

To this end I'm wearing a charcoal Armani suit with a fine pinstripe, a white linen shirt from Ede and Ravenscroft—which has remained miraculously uncreased—and a maroon silk Pucci tie. Lucia looks splendid in her dark blue Ralph Lauren Collection trouser suit—*very* smart, and with a touch of attitude— a plain white tailored man's shirt by Dior and a pair of slightly intimidating Prada ankle boots that lend a good four inches to her height. We've both got smart leather flight cases neatly packed with expensive casual wear, chic underclothes, a laptop, an iPad, the requisite toiletries and, in Lucia's, a compact but curiously robust vibrator. She insists that if we come under scrutiny it will divert and dilute any unwanted attention. Well, OK. As long as it's in her case and not mine.

I'm not sure why but neither of us appears anxious. Perhaps it's because we've lived so long in such peculiar and adverse circumstances that we no longer respond normally. Suffice to say, if you imagine that I'm *not* smuggling a felonious amount of ultra high-grade coke into this formerly hard line communist country, and if you imagine that we're *not* going all-in on this last turn of the cards, you'll have a better idea of our combined demeanor.

It's our turn. We step forward together. The smart young officer sends me back.

Suddenly it feels like I've got a bag of sugar stuffed down the back of my trousers. A wave of heat sweeps through my chest and up to my forehead. It's not a hot day so I hope I'm not going to start sweating. That would be…

difficult. I watch carefully as he studies her passport and runs through his drill. Lucia is smiling earnestly, nodding her understanding, offering some words of explanation, managing to look both confident and demure. Great show. But for all that, he wants to look in her flight case. Not good. I'm beginning to prepare myself for the same treatment. Breathing slowly and deeply. Running through our story. Going over the small print. He's foraging thoroughly, albeit politely, through her things. He stops, his hands deep in the case. He looks closely at something, looks up at Lucia, back again, then at me. Carefully and precisely he repacks her things, snaps the locks shut, then stamps and hands back her passport. He smiles and executes a small bow and extends his arm towards the exit.

He looks at me again, motions me forward and takes a brief look at my own passport. He stamps it, dips an eyelid in what might be the slightest of winks and ushers me after her. I thank him and catch up.

"Told you," she says, swinging her hips slightly.

The electric gates swish open and suddenly we're in Niš. Beyond immigration there is the usual press of people scanning faces, looking at watches, waving hands and parading names and notices while waiting for colleagues, friends, family, lovers and, hopefully, an experimental drug trial subject. Lucia nudges my arm and discreetly points towards a burly man in a tight black jacket, black jeans and Doc Martens shoes. He's holding a small placard with 'Mr./Mrs. Russell' printed in large bold type. Amidst the slowly churning throng, there's a noticeable perimeter around him. We start in his direction and, though he's not looking anywhere in particular, I reckon that he's clocked us. As we step across the threshold of his force field I sense a frisson in the crowd around us, an unconscious sigh perhaps, or a collective intake of breath. His bullet head rotates like a turret and hard eyes fix on mine. I'm about to put my hand out in greeting but my reflexes tell me it's a waste of time. Lucia reaches for our passports and holds them to his gaze. He glances at them briefly and inclines his head towards the main exit.

"Poḑite sa mnom molim", he says quietly but clearly. I don't understand him but the meaning is clear. We follow him, the crowd yielding to either side of his trajectory, and step out of the terminal into a bright, cool day. Parked on the curb directly opposite is a new electric Mercedes saloon which, despite its sleek bulk, can do five hundred miles between charges.

Nice.

The trunk swings open as we arrive and he points at it. Much as I would rather hang onto my things, this really doesn't feel like the moment to rock the boat. We put our flight cases in its capacious interior, though Lucia pointedly retains her handbag. The man looks at it, then nods curtly and shuts them away. Gesticulating towards Lucia, he opens the nearside door, more to ensure that we get in than for any reasons of etiquette, I suspect, though he leaves me to move around the car and let myself in. Then he joins us and silently the big car moves off. The locks click shut.

Instead of heading east towards the city, we start westwards, picking up speed as we turn south on the A1. Within minutes, we've left the glass and concrete of the airport behind as the empty highway traces its way through the bucolic hinterland of rural Serbia. Despite—or perhaps because of—the pulp fiction drama of our arrival, I feel focused and alert now that we've arrived at the final act. I reach over for Lucia's hand and relax, preparing to settle into the journey. Her fingers are cool and reassuring and I begin to consider our next move, but after barely ten minutes we come upon a cluster of gleaming new buildings —warehouses, offices and light manufacturing units— collectively announced as the "Donje Medurovo Free Zone" by their gaudy advertising billboards. We slow down, turn on to a service road and draw up to a gated checkpoint. Without any apparent exchange the barrier rises and we're in. The driver threads his way through the lattice of access roads and driveways and pulls up to a smart entrance—a sweeping curve of industrial steel and tinted glass— though otherwise unadorned except for a discreet silver nameplate lettered in Cyrillic. On closer inspection, I notice that it's accompanied by a smaller Roman font indicating our arrival at the Phuture PharmaTherapies Testing Facility.

Neither of us have said a word.

Lucia

It's been a long ride. Marc double-dosed this morning and topped up with a discreet but substantial supplement of cocaine shortly before we began our descent into Niš. I think he'll hold out sufficiently to provide Professor Gaynes with the evidence he'll be looking for. I don't like it but Marc and I have agreed that he will relapse in their presence. I will supervise any observations they wish to make.

And now we're here.

I've not booked anywhere to stay tonight because I want to press our advantage, so I hope we'll be welcome— or at least sufficiently compelling—to stick around, though I have no way of knowing if we'll be either. In truth, I feel a little frightened. More than a little, in fact. The accumulating impact of living on my wits and adrenaline is exhausting and I'm beginning to worry about whether, or more likely when I'll founder. The border check came close. I wanted just to scream or cry or lay down. When

Marc took my hand in the car, his was so warm. Mine was still cold with shock.

And now we're here.

I've tried to plan for everything. I've tried to manage everything. I've tried to put on my bravest face. But this next part contains too many unknowns and so we'll have to improvise. I hope we're both up to it.

Because now we are here.

Our driver—a sinister man who exudes menace and barely suppressed violence—comes around and opens my door. I breathe deeply, then glance at Marc and smile. It's automatic, this need to provide reassurance though it dawns on me that—increasingly—it is mostly for my own benefit. He smiles back and gestures towards my exit as he leans towards his own. We alight and converge on the entrance, joining up as we arrive at the threshold. The driver is behind us.

He doesn't have our bags.

Again, the automatic doors cleave before us and we step forward through our increasingly fractured reality into...

... a bright atrium. It's illuminated by broad shafts of afternoon sunlight, each channeled through one of four large slabs of tempered glass recessed into the gently sloping roof. In front of us, across an expanse of spotless marbled flooring, there is yet another pair of automated doors, this time made of what looks like security grade stainless steel. They're flanked by a pair of touchscreens set into white high-gloss wall paneling. On our right, there is an expansive grey suede sofa preceded by a Monobloc glass and concrete coffee table. A sophisticated black and chrome coffee machine is set into an alcove nearby. To our left, there is an elegant kidney-shaped reception desk fashioned out of the palest ash. Its only adornment is a big iMac—unless, I suppose, you count the platinum blond Valkyrie tapping away at her keyboard. I can't imagine she doesn't know who we are but I guess we all have our role; she duly adopts hers.

"Nem, plis." She looks at us expectantly, fingers poised over the keys. What the hell.

"I'm Lucia Russell. This is my husband, Marc. We're here to see Professors Gaynes and Mbengwe." She clicks away, apparently entering this information into her system. Marc says nothing.

"Ah, yes, plis. Mr. and Mrs. Russell. We expecting you. Is good flight you have? Perhaps you like coffee? Or prefer tea? Sit, plis. I bring." She comes out from behind her barricade and directs us to the sofa as she makes her way to the fancy drinks dispenser. "Professors being with you soon," she calls over her shoulder. "Now, what you drink?"

I ask for two cups of tea. One each.

"Yes, you British drinking always tea. Serbians preferring always coffee. Excepting old people with Samovar. Drink tea too but, we not have." She looks momentarily crestfallen, but then brightens. "Machine making tea also, hope you like." She taps in our order and it begins to hiss and burble. "My name is Dušana, you call Ana, plis." She brings our tea over. It is pale and has no milk, though she has put two sachets of sugar on each saucer.

"Thank you. Ana, where are our bags, do you know?" I open all four sachets and stir them into my pale tea. Marc sips at his.

"Bogdan take them to lab." She makes a face. "Bogdan is driver. You not go now. Staying, yes? Ah, look," she points at the steel security doors. A red light is blinking above them and the touchscreens read 'Cycling...' The three dots flash sequentially while a progress bar flows gradually across the bottom of the display.

"Professors coming now! Soon meet!" For a moment she looks extremely pleased with herself as though she has personally conjured them into being, then returns to her work station and makes herself busy.

There is a melodious chime. I stand up and turn slightly towards the doors. Marc puts his cup on the coffee table and sits back. The flashing red light changes to a solid green. The touchscreens read "Cycling complete."

The doors slide back into their recesses.

Marc

Professors Gaynes and Mbengwe step from their airlock into the light and air of the atrium. While Lucia stands to meet them, I shift just enough to place them in my field of vision, though I'm careful not to look at them directly just yet. I don't want them to be able to gauge my present disposition. It may serve to heighten the effect of my transformation, bearing in mind that their only exposure to my condition, by contact or report, will have been as someone suffering from classic Alzheimer's.

Professor Gaynes looks nervous though this doesn't stop his eyes flickering over Lucia's body, pausing momentarily to measure her tits behind the taut material of her Dior shirt. Maybe he's got a thing for blacks, regardless of sex. It happens. By contrast, Mbengwe looks entirely relaxed, a broad grin on his handsome, chiseled features. He really is quite beautiful. Long almond-shaped eyes taper upwards at their outer corners. The eyes themselves are that curious light green that occasionally occurs in black people. The rest of his eyes—and his teeth—are spectacularly white in contrast with his dark skin, which is much darker than Lucia's. His head and face are clean shaven. He is tall, lean and poised, possessed of the coiled grace of an athlete.

He's wearing a white collarless shirt buttoned to the neck, and a black suit.

He looks great.

For all this, and despite the smile, his green eyes are cold, hard, and utterly calculating as he takes a long look at each of us. Professor Gaynes seems about to speak, but it is Mbengwe who breaks the silence.

"Mr. and Mrs. Russell, I presume?" His voice is rich and cultured, his accent the modern form of Received Pronunciation, absent of any apparent trace of his African upbringing. He focuses his attention entirely on Lucia but makes no further move to greet her. Professor Gaynes looks from one to the other, his nervousness seeming to escalate. An uncomfortable silence extends for a moment; then, just as Mbengwe seems about to pursue his overture, his smile diminishing, Lucia steps forward, hand extended, and greets them both.

"Professor Mbengwe, Charles, thank you so much for inviting us both. It's a real pleasure to be here. I do hope we can work together." Her hand hovers for a moment, then Mbengwe takes it, his grin suddenly back in place. Surprisingly he lifts it to his lips and brushes them across her fingers, his green eyes narrowed and appraising.

"That depends. I'm not yet precisely clear what you're offering. That is why you are here, to provide clarity. Your narrative, as Charles explained it to me, is remarkably accurate and your assessment rings true. You are quite correct in your judgment that my back is up against the wall. Do not press me further to it. It's true, I do have much to lose so a little more won't hurt if push comes to shove. Serbia is still a lawless place, in many respects."

I wonder if Lucia will acknowledge the implied threat.

"Ah yes, of course. There is that side of things. I've brought you both a copy of our report. Perhaps you already have it? It was in our bags. It's mostly complete and I doubt our hacker will have left anything by which you can trace him. There's a further copy, unabridged, lodged with my attorney. It is, I realize, only modest insurance and I don't suppose it will count for much if we suffer a falling out. Still, it *will* go to the authorities."

Gaynes looks utterly petrified as Lucia calmly introduces this contingency into the conversation. Mbengwe looks momentarily stricken, and then his urbanity slips: his lips peel back against his bared teeth and his eyes widen and bulge. His shoulders hunch and his hands reach towards Lucia's throat. He is actually growling. I should act, but no, I won't. He won't strike, yet. I'll hang on to our leverage, just as we agreed. I continue to stare into the middle distance; the fool, the foil.

In the midst of the standoff, Dušana continues to type, her word count positively Olympic as the tension stretches to breaking point.

"But I'm sure it won't come to that," Lucia continues, seemingly unperturbed, emollient, her voice like honey. "Let's concentrate instead on how to make things work. It's probably time you had a word with my husband." Amazingly, she takes Mbengwe's outstretched hands in her own and presses them together, as she speaks, then lowers them to his sides.

"Perhaps that will give us the perspective we need."

Lucia

God, this is hard. I thought he was going to strangle me with his bare hands. I've never seen such bestial savagery in a face. I said earlier that the airport was a challenge, a trial. It was kindergarten by comparison. We're going deeper down the rabbit hole, deeper and faster, suddenly and irrevocably. My pathetic "insurance" won't mean a thing if Mbengwe goes psycho on me again. The membrane between man and beast is too thin, too permeable. He'll take everything down once he concludes it's all over. Maybe he has a bolt-hole, maybe not. The point is, he just won't care. It's everything or nothing with this one. I've got to give him everything. Our job is to help him win. That way we live and Marc will live better. It's worth every scintilla of anxiety, pain and fear, now that we're here.

So far Marc has kept to our script. Saying nothing, doing nothing. Staring blankly into space, slightly slumped, poor body tone. It's what we agreed, to emphasize the contrast when he does his big reveal. And now we've got the formalities out of the way, well, it's time for Marc to do his thing.

"It's probably time you had a word with my husband," I say, taking Mbengwe's murderous hands in my own and pressing them together, then lowering them to his sides. The violence drains out of his expression. "Perhaps that will give us the perspective we need." I turn slightly to include Marc in our proceedings.

"I can't see what use that's going to be. He appears to be barely aware." Mbengwe clenches his jaw and breathes in deeply, reminding himself, perhaps, that he's out of options. "Well, I suppose we should do some basics if we're to take this seriously. Charles, what do you make of him?"

"I'm not sure Nicholas, he appears fairly withdrawn. Better dressed than I've seen him to be sure. Perhaps we could baseline him with one of the newer cognitive tests I've been…"

"I don't think that's going to be necessary, gentlemen," Marc interrupts, rising and turning to face them. He rolls his shoulders, flexing to loosen himself up, then draws himself to his full height. Did I ever mention he's a good six feet? Slim but powerful?

He looks great.

"We're in the Donje Medurovo Free Zone," he continues, "and it's now around four-thirty pm on Monday 27th May in the year of our good Lord twenty-nineteen. That's two-zero-one-nine. Your excellent receptionist is named Dušana but prefers that we call her Ana. Your less than civil driver is referred to as Bogdan, which can be roughly translated from the Serbian as "given from God". You'll forgive me if I make no comment. At present, there is developing concern in Western capitals that the Iranian government has managed to covertly install a substantial number of additional, state-of-the-art centrifuges in the Natanz and Fordo uranium enrichment facilities. That's in direct contravention of the Joint Comprehensive Plan of Action agreed back in July 2015... how'm I doing? Is that good enough for the baseline? We've done place, time, recall, detail, current events – I reckon it must be worth at least an eight on the scorecard. I can draw the hours on a clock if you insist...?"

Fantastic! After all their supercilious arrogance and callous intimidation, they look like a pair of schoolboys, each caught with other's cock in his hand. Mouths agape, bug-eyed and disbelieving, they seem unable to come to terms with this new reality. Suddenly it's feeling easier to handle things. I'll just imagine them with their zippers down, genitals dangling and impotent, caught in ludicrous flagrante delicto.

As if to reinforce their capitulation, they begin to argue with each other. Mbengwe goes first:

"You said, and I quote, 'that he was suffering from moderate to severe dementia presenting primarily as extreme apathy though punctuated by bouts of aggression driven or exacerbated by persistent underlying anxiety'. I fail to see any of..."

"I also said that his CAT and MRI scans showed atypical progression, indeed no progression at all in some respects..." Gaynes blusters.

"So what the bloody hell is going on here, he's more articulate than you, for fuck's sake. We need..."

"Yes," Marc interrupts again, "you need to take a good look. I'm fine with that. As Professor Mbengwe said earlier, that is why I'm here. My only demand, and it is an absolute condition, is that Lucia remains with me at all stages. Shortly—probably in less than an hour, maybe much less than an hour—you'll witness something quite unusual. I will, spontaneously and completely, retreat to the condition you've been expecting. No doubt you'll want to put your splendid scanners to work. I imagine they're somewhat underused to date, what with the fatality and all."

I wish he'd not said that last bit and for a moment I hold my breath; the last thing I want is to provoke Mbengwe further. But it seems I needn't worry. They barely miss a beat. I think they're hooked.

"Do you have any insight into how you've managed this... this... well, this frankly miraculous feat?" asks Gaynes, still incredulous.

"Yes... yes I do. It's all down to bad living and a serious cocaine habit." The two scientists look bemused. "Look, I've written some notes. It all centers on the CART transcript. I... what the hell, they're yours if we can come to an agreement. Lucia, tell them. Your proposition. I think it's almost time."

Again the focus comes back to me. I no longer mind. Marc has played his part, now this is mine.

"Actually it's simple. I have a contract. It sets out Marc's intention to be the willing subject, for three years, of your research to establish how he has survived this ordeal and how it can be exploited to help others. You will administer to him, as soon as possible, but within the first three months of this, the first year, the Mabetamine and Limenofil compound using the Harmonized Oscillatory Resonance Reaction. I presume Algernon is here, or will be available?" Slight nods, and Gaynes' eyes flick to the steel airlock. "Good. I suppose the sooner the better really, because people are going to begin enquiring as to what has happened here quite soon, I imagine. The quicker we get the real story up and running the better for all of us.

"Anyway, I will be with Marc at every stage. You will explain whatever avenues you are exploring to me and Marc and you will abide by our decisions as to whether they advance, which will not be unreasonably withheld. If Marc is indisposed, I will make those decisions.

"After that we will agree, for the second year, to monthly consultations each lasting two days. After that, in the third and final year of our contract, the consultations will be quarterly, again for two days each time. Within this period, we will submit to further ad-hoc consultations at our discretion. Marc agrees to exemplify your work to whoever needs to validate it, for the duration of the contract.

"You will pay us consultancy fees at a flat rate of two thousand dollars per day—each—during all of this time and when it's over, it's over. We want no money, we want no celebrity, and we don't even want any recognition if we can help it. The glory and success are all yours. The world might be a better place. That's up to you.

"What do you say?"

"Well, of course we'll need to consider this contract of yours," Gaynes begins, "and we certainly can't afford..." With a weary and unexpected tenderness Mbengwe puts his hand on Gaynes' arm, stopping him.

"Yes. I say yes."

I look to Marc for his approval, but he's gone. Down. Down to his depths.

Chapter Twenty-Three

Marc and Lucia

Marc

I've been here a couple of months now. In Niš, I mean. Full summer has arrived and it's very hot outside, the Free Zone and the surrounding country sweltering in a plume of hot, dry air blown up from the Sahara. It's taken root over southeastern Europe, sustained by a ridge of high pressure parked stubbornly over the Mediterranean.

Why the weather forecast? You might well ask. It's because the weather is the only other thing I really get to notice these days, and that's mostly from behind glass. The rest of the time, maybe half of my waking hours, is spent in one or other of the two big scanners parked in the principal observation suite, out back through the airlock. There's no one else here except the professors, Algernon (who comes and goes), Lucia, Dušana and bloody Bogdan who scares Lucia and irritates me. A high powered Polish nurse called Małgorzata, who insists that we call her Goska, completes our limited society. The previous occupants, whoever they were, have gone. I don't know where. I haven't asked.

Lucia and I effectively live here. The facility was originally set up to test and monitor twelve subjects so it's quite large. Mbengwe and Gaynes both have a room for when our work runs late, though they also have neighboring apartments in town. Algernon also has a room here and I understand he shares Mbengwe's apartment at other times though, as I said, he comes and goes. We're looked after—and politely but carefully monitored—by Bogdan and Dušana, one or other of whom is with us 24/7. Their schedule is inscrutable, however, and it's hard to know who will be on duty when. Małgorzata mainly interacts with the professors and, while very much part of the team when on duty, otherwise keeps herself to herself.

Lucia and Dušana have become good friends. They've been out together a few times – sightseeing, or to bars and coffee shops. I'm glad, because otherwise I suppose we'd both be going mad. Lucia tells me about their outings, and about Ana, and she passes on the gossip that Ana chooses to share. She's also been showing her how to use spreadsheets and pivot tables to analyze some of the data I'm producing, and I've been producing plenty, believe me. That's the main reason I'm stuck here, in the observation suite and its ancillary rooms. I need to live in a regulated environment so that all the many tests, myriad experiments, abundant observations and numerous investigations are comparable and properly controlled. We don't have a control group, not even a control subject. It's just me, so I'm the constant.

I understand they're also looking at how to synthesize the CART protein and Algernon is doing his weird drug-bloodhound thing, using his singular talent to parse the millions of folds that make the protein work. I guess he's looking to see if he can optimize it to go further than just preserve the synapse. I mean, good luck to them— that's an unexpected payoff, an area they'd not even considered.

More recently, there has been a number of visits by some other academic luminaries who have spent a lot of time going over the data. I have the impression their purpose is to confirm findings and record progress; to invigilate, as it were. One time there was a something of a carnival atmosphere that seemed to accompany their stay. After a busy week revisiting a particular batch of tests, presumably to confirm their repeatability—the gold standard of scientific method, there was a lot of handshaking and backslapping, then they all went off to lunch, leaving Lucia and me under the not especially watchful eye of Ana. We managed to have sex that afternoon. I won't go into the details this time, but it was marvelous, and much needed.

The good news is that I've got a steady supply of the purest cocaine. The bad news is I only get to have it when they let me, and then I'm usually in the scanner, or wired up to the diagnostics, or both. There's some other good news too, in that they're keeping to their side of the bargain on the money front. Lucia keeps an eye on things. It's clocking up nicely in an offshore dollar account she set up to accommodate our substantial wages.

In fact, the professors have never been less than professional, though I'm afraid we're never going to be best friends. Our courtship was way too turbulent for that. But they're inevitably courteous and occasionally even kind. Mbengwe—I still can't call him Nicholas—is mostly friendly but I figure that's how most sociopaths are when things are going their way and yes, things are mostly going his way. He and Charles (yes, I do sometimes call him Charles—he's my doctor after all, we virtually live together and he's not actually a psycho) are on a roll. Now that they've confirmed my basic premise, they've established that I've suffered very little, if any, long term pathological deterioration. We're on the cusp of the money shot. If their therapy works, I guess they're going to be able to say they've cured Alzheimer's. If only in me.

And that's what I've mostly been leading up to. Tomorrow's the day. Tomorrow they're going to administer the first clinical dose of the Alpha-Mabetamine and Limenofil-X7 compound. They've tried several sub-therapeutic doses to test my tolerance and scanned for any potential side effects. So far there have been none, but they remain cautious.

Rightly so. It's my brain.

In an ideal world, I think they'd have preferred to push the main event to the very end of the three month period we agreed, but they've brought it forward. There have been complications.

They were whispered by Ana to Lucia on a recent girls' night out. They're not technical. They're not even medical. I suppose you might call them procedural, or administrative, but really they're legal, and probably criminal. They're the basis for Lucia's original strategy for getting me here, now floating ominously to the surface. They're the skeletons in our closet. The crows coming home to roost.

They began with a call from one of the Free Zone trustees, explaining that Her Majesty's Revenue and Customs had been asking some questions about British investments in the area. This had been followed by some very general enquiries about the filing of local Clinical Trial applications with the European Medicines Agency and then, rather more pointedly, a request to ALIMS—the responsible authority in Serbia—for the re-submission of all their recent applications direct to the EU Clinical Trials Registry.

These look to me like clear signs that the shit will soon hit the fan, very much along the lines that Lucia predicted in her conversation with Charles shortly before we came here. And now, as Lucia also advised shortly thereafter... "The quicker we get the real story up and running the better for all of us."

So tomorrow it is.

Lucia

Today's the day. Tomorrow we'll know how everything is going to be. For now, the fear is enormous. And I wasn't expecting this:

Marc looks as if he's fallen prey to a particularly obsessive and covetous spider. He's lying supine in the barrel of the MRI scanner, meticulously laced into a complex lattice of tubes, wires and straps that secure him at the epicenter of a sprawling network of pumps, computers and visual displays. His recently shaven head is held rigid by a sinister web-like restraint. Four micro-catheter arrays have been embedded in his skull. Though the Mabetamine and Limenofil compound crosses from the bloodstream into the brain, these can be used to deliver additional targeted doses.

They remind me of tiny oil rigs on a model globe.

The rest of the principal observation suite looks like the mission control center of a space launch. A collection of flat screen monitors is suspended from the ceiling, radiating an unceasing torrent of real time clinical and biological data to the team, now seated at their four workstations ranged around the scanner.

Marc is, of course, deeply unconscious, already long into this, his final frontier. Nurse Małgorzata is posted just to his right, roughly level with his shoulders, observing his vital signs through her battery of displays. She's in charge of a cluster of sophisticated medical, operational, and life-support systems including the cutting-edge expert system that she's using to micromanage the anesthesia. She exudes the poise and assurance of a trained professional in the midst of her flow.

To Marc's left, nearest his immobile head, is Professor Mbengwe. He's staring intently at a massive, curving display, calibrating the scanner so that he can quickly toggle between different locations and depths of field. Right now he is cycling through high definition images of the minutely positioned delivery apertures of the micro-catheters. The instruments, sunk deep in Marc's brain, seem besieged by ominous clumps of beta-amyloid – ugly tangled masses of deformed protein, each with its dark halo of toxins and debris.

They are the enemy.

Stationed next to him, also to Marc's left, is Algernon Benacerrafi. Though he's much older now, he looks strangely untouched—his ascetic features and serene expression still reminiscent of the messiah that Donna Fulbright once described. His own display unit appears to be slaved to Mbengwe's but with several different data streams scrolling at absurd speeds across a virtual overlay. I'm told that he processes them almost reflexively, responding to events with tactical precision as the procedure evolves. His fingers trip lightly over the controls, rehearsing the moves that will cure my husband.

Professor Gaynes is in pole position, gazing directly into the sleekly curving muzzle of the machine. His own workstation is relatively uncluttered, just a laptop, a secondary keyboard and, surprisingly, a thick sheaf of handwritten notes highlighted with luminous yellow and pink marker. He's got line of sight with all of the others and his watchful eyes flicker between the overhead monitors and his colleagues. His job is to coordinate the therapeutic and clinical elements of the operation, and just as Mbengwe is the charismatic leader of this team, Gaynes is the link man, the unassuming manager, the team's backstop. One by one, as the initial checks are confirmed, he screws up the notes and tosses them over his shoulder.

I resist the urge to reach out and catch them. I'm seated just behind him, feeling entirely redundant. I would have waited it out, if I'd had to, but Marc insisted I was here, and I'm glad.

The crumpled notes gradually build up around me.

All of us are wearing full surgical kits. We're also fully rigged with noise cancelling headphones and throat mikes. The scanner is cacophonous, like a cross between a buzz-saw and a jackhammer but the earphones are remarkably effective, silencing the appalling racket and replacing it with the calm tones and structural perfection of a Bach sonata. It's unsurprising that surgical teams enjoy working to music, though there is a vigorous debate as to what works best. Listening in, as an uninvolved observer, I can see how the mathematical harmonies and cadences contribute to an atmosphere of calm focus. Occasional exchanges of technical conversation punctuate the score, usually terminated with a terse "Check" or "Proceed" from Gaynes as another of his notes bites the dust.

Finally satisfied with his status checks, Mbengwe confirms his own readiness. Without ceremony or fanfare, Gaynes starts the procedure.

"OK people, we're ready. Algernon, on my mark, start the primary infusion. Goska, can I have EEG and cardio on two please? Nicholas, please keep an eye on plasma levels and be wary of cytokine feedback. Ok Algernon, ready... go."

And that's it. A certain stiffening of awareness, a couple of controls minutely adjusted and it's make or break time.

"Good, all signs nominal. Goska, Algernon, I'm looking for titration point alpha. Give me the curve on three please. OK. Thanks. Algernon, on my mark. Start the secondary infusion. Curve is good. Counting back from five... four... three... two... and go.

"Nicholas, I'm looking for initial nano-scale erosion. Try your preset gamma-two-delta on screen four at full magnification. Algernon, I'm expecting the oscillatory resonance to begin its first harmonic any time soon. I'm waiting... OK, mark. Good. Nicholas, have you got anything?"

"Charles, yes, I can see initial dispersion. It's minute, but it's happening. Goska, can you amplify plasma and send Algernon the feed? Good. Algernon, cut the infusion to seventy percent. I want to try saturation on catheter sixteen. I'm looking for micro-scale erosion..."

"Careful Nicholas, I think we should wait for titration point beta. Algernon hold. Nicholas hold. Goska, display the curve at maximum resolution. Yes, good. Algernon, Nicholas, deploy on my mark. Three... two ... one... go. OK. You're on. Nicholas, Goska, I'm getting minor fluctuations in cytokine density. Take it easy. The last thing we want is another positive loop."

Oops. They're going to have to edit that from the record. The words begin to wash over me. I feel sleepy, hypnotized by the music and the drab technicalities of paradigm shift. I think, translated, that what they're saying is that those awful bundles of broken shit in Marc's brain are getting the kicking they deserve. That after years of their insidious attempts at undermining our happy ever after, the big guns of science and reason are about to kick out the jams from under their godforsaken evolutionary sideshow and make way for life and progress. History in the making and my husband being brought, bit by bit, back to me.

I just want it to be over.

But no. Something's wrong. Professor Gaynes has interrupted the procedure. Suddenly I'm wide awake.

"Wait, pull back. Stop. There's a hyperactive immune response developing, potentially hyperbolic. Cut primary and secondary infusions to fifty percent. No, better make the twenty. Goska, we've practiced this in vitro, OK? Remember it works in the models so *don't* hesitate. Give me COX-2 inhibitor and PAF inception as indicated in alpha-three contingency, now please, quickly...

"OK, it's not working. Cardio is showing red and plasma is approaching saturation. This is bad. Wait.

"OK. This is what we'll do. Maintain alpha-three and introduce vagal stimulation. Yes. Do it. Algernon, return to seventy percent, I'm looking for your second harmonic. Now if you don't mind. Don't fuck about, make it happen. We can't lose the impetus. Goska the curve's going critical, increase the vagal stimulation and launch the GTS-21 program. Yes, both, and yes, now. No time to waste Goska. Go.

"Jesus, cardio is at 160bpm. Goska, Algernon, are you running? Yes? We're up to 165. The curve's tapering but his rate isn't. One-seventy... one-seventy-two... one-seventy-one... Ok we're down to one-six-eight, one-sixty, it's coming down nicely, the curve's dipping. Looking better. Nicholas, have we still got erosion?"

"Yes, Charles, while you've all been jumping around, I've begun to get macro scale erosion. We should see renal effects soon. I think we should be concentrating on the secondary infusion and the third harmonic. That is if you're sure he's not going to die? Hmmm?"

"Nick, just shut the fuck up. We've got to get the immune response sorted or we're not going to be winning any Nobel prizes any time soon. But no, he's not going to die. Put your flush data on two please. Wow... that's impressive. He'll be pissing beta-amyloid soon. The third phase shift is stable. Any data on neuron function?"

"Yes, actually. I've got increasing potential across cholinergic pathways and some evidence of increasing ACh activity. I'm also beginning to get readings confirming decline in AChE levels, not quite conforming to our models yet, but definitely trending. I'm routing it to monitor five so you can all get a look. But here's the killer. Look. I've got decreasing potential across all P75 neurodegenerative channels. The curves are beginning to synchronize. Fortification is looking very good. How's the immune response? I think we should activate all of the remaining pumps starting at twenty percent. What do you say, Charles?"

"I say wait until all our data is stable. Goska, show me the immune response in real time please. I must say that's looking very good but keep the contingencies primed. We'll wait thirty minutes. Sorry, but I'm not losing another."

They hadn't better. Nor ought they to leave that on the record either. I'd better put them in touch with our hacker. At least my heart's beginning to quieten as the panic recedes. I look at monitor two, where Mbengwe's has projected his image of the hateful amyloid mass encroaching on the catheters. As the minutes tick by, I notice its halo of poisonous material gradually dispersing. Even as it dissipates, it dawns on me that one of the smaller lumps of protein is actually shrinking. It's like watching an effervescent tablet in slow motion: gradually the edge of the clump thins, then fractures, then breaks away, casting off smaller fragments of protein which, in turn, split and splinter until they eventually fizzle away to nothing. Mbengwe reduces the magnification and I can see it happening on an ever-larger scale, like a great battlefield where pockets of surrender suddenly become a rout on every front. Suddenly Professor Gaynes speaks again.

"OK Nicholas, I think we can cautiously include the rest of cluster four. Activate catheters thirteen through fifteen. Twenty percent to start. Let's see the progress. My goodness, that is good. Excellent in fact. We'll give it fifteen minutes then work through the rest."

Stage by stage the rout continues, the amyloid retreating as the onslaught consolidates. Mbengwe continues to broadcast his steady stream of good news, our mantra of hope: amyloid clear, neural potentials recovering, neurotrophic signaling normalized.

Eventually, after some six hours of unrelenting concentration, of the grueling extremities of ardent hope and abject fear and then the final, soaring realization that we've succeeded, Professor Gaynes throws the last crumpled note over his shoulder.

I catch it, like a bridesmaid clutching at fortune.

After a moment, he closes his laptop and looks at each of the team, then finally at me. "Ladies and gentlemen, well done. Mrs. Russell, thank you for helping to bring us to this point. We might not have otherwise have had this chance.

"We can't be certain yet, of course, but – I think we've done it.

"I think we've cured Alzheimer's."

Chapter Twenty-Four

The Inhibitionist

That all happened just under three years ago.

Things are different now. First off, they did cure Alzheimer's disease... mine. I couldn't grasp it at first. It was like I had to pull together these two disparate personalities who had developed along such different paths. The slow one, he knew stuff. Stuff I didn't. The quick one—he did stuff. Stuff I coulldn't.

Oops.

Couldn't.

But, you know what it's like to focus binoculars? Did you ever do that? It's like you've got two

different, blurry pictures
in the lenses, then as you
adjust the alignment and
the focal point—bam! They
suddenly come together in
spectacular detail. That's
how it seemed to me and
the focal point was Lucia.
Me and him, or him and me,
both understood at our
deepest levels who she was
and what she meant.
Bringing and blending
those two things together
was the trick. Unlike a
lot of therapy, it was
always a pleasure, never a
chore.

Obviously I've knocked the
coke on the head, though I
sometimes quaff the
occasional modafinil if I
need to get over some hump
or other. I'm pretty good

at thinking *around* things but I've still got some blockers that can stop me dead for a day, and every little bit helps. Nor am I sure that I'm as smart as I used to be, I mean before all of this happened, but man, have I got perspective.

Oh, by the way, do you know I never saw Yakov or Natassja again? After that weird evening in Soho? I suppose I didn't need to given how things turned out, but... I don't know. Call it a loose end.

I called by. They weren't there. The building had been gutted, just the Regency façade left intact. I thought about our last conversation: I think, now, that it was just the coke and coincidence—the unlikely intersection of people worlds apart.

I suppose you're wondering what happened to the professors and Algernon. They flourished. The coke thing provided a whole new avenue for Algernon to do his stuff. Last I heard, he'd developed some kind of analogue with all of the CART properties, maxed out of course, but none of the buzz. It's in phase two trials and causing a stir.

But of course, the main event was my cure. Yes it hit the headlines. Yes, it rocketed them all to star status. And yes, it enabled the authorities to forget any inconvenient truths that might have cropped up.

For a while, I had more academics than you could shake a stick at poring all over me. They were often cynical, jealous bastards just looking for a flaw.

But there were none.

I was ill, I got treated, and I got better. End of story. For what it's worth, the odds are on the three of them to share the Nobel Prize for Medicine this coming December, the year of our Lord 2022. I wish them well.

Our contract worked out just fine. We cleared around two million dollars which, given the outrageous interest rates these days, has pulled in a tidy premium. On top of that, Lucia had first dibs on stock in the (properly incorporated) Phuture Pharma Therapies (UK) Limited.

We're really quite rich now.

Lucia's fine, and we're still tight together. We live in Florida at the moment. We've got a house down there.

She sends her love.

Oh, I don't really need to write in big letters anymore either, but, you know, for old time's sake.

Ciao.

Postscript: Extracts from Marc's notes

"In 1995, Douglass *et al.* found that a particular mRNA was upregulated by acute administration of **cocaine or amphetamine**. They named this transcript **'cocaine- and amphetamine-regulated transcript' (CART)**. The transcript is usually referred to as CART mRNA, and the encoded peptides are referred to as CART peptides."

"CART level is also reduced in AD patients. The precise mechanisms of CART underlining these changes and the significance of CART in both DLB and AD diseases need further investigation in the future..."

"Although the involvement of CART in mitochondria and neurotrophic signaling in healthy and injured neurons is increasingly recognized, **the impact of CART on the cellular processing of amyloid precursor protein tau and alpha-synuclein, the key genes/proteins associated AD and DLB, is currently unexplored...**"

"CART is a well-characterized neuropeptide with the capacity to modulate body weight and alcohol consumption. Recently, protection against cellular degeneration, which is an alternative CART function, has received growing attention, although studies in this area are still limited. In a previous in vitro study by the current study team, it was discovered that **upregulation of CART... reduced the death rate of cultured cortical neurons in response to Aβ toxicity.**"

"The present study elucidates the effects of CART treatment on memory deficits and synaptic loss in APP/PS1 transgenic mice. The study found that **CART treatment**

significantly attenuated memory deficits. Injections of exogenous CART re-established synaptic ultrastructure in the cortex and hippocampus, increased synapse numbers, and preserved LTP. CART also mitigated potential for depolarization of the mitochondrial membrane, a major cause of mitochondrial dysfunction, possibly by its ability to reduce intracellular ROS and lipid peroxidation and to decrease mitochondrial (mtDNA) oxidative damage."

"**Notably, oxidative damage is thought to be the earliest event in Alzheimer's disease**. Aβ directly induces reactive oxygen species (ROS), and toxic soluble Aβ oligomers appear to have synaptic receptors colocalizing with PSD-95 (postsynaptic density protein 95), and Aβ42 accumulates in dendrites in AD patients where it may cause oxidative damage and caspase activation and eventually apoptosis [30]. On the other hand, mitochondrial dysfunction and mitochondria-derived ROS lead to enhanced Aβ formation. **Therefore, a vicious cycle starting either from mitochondrial dysfunction or Aβ toxicity is triggered** that contributes to the pathogenesis of the most AD and the mitochondrial cascade hypothesis is increasingly recognized, especially for the most common form, later onset of AD."

"**Results suggest that the mechanisms underlying CART-mediated neuroprotection include attenuation of oxidative damage and improvement of mitochondrial function. These findings support the notion that CART-based therapies may be beneficial in AD patients.**"

"In the current study, CART was shown to improve structure of neurites and reduce ROS, 8-OHdG and 4-HNE levels, two robust indicators of oxidative stress, and these changes were associated with improved mitochondrial function, consistent with published reports. **These results** suggest that CART has the capacity to counter neuronal oxidative stress and mitochondrial dysfunction. Therefore, the accumulation of CART in Aβ plaques may serve as a compensatory mechanism to delay degenerative processes in dystrophic neurites and suppress Aβ plaque toxicity. Because neuritic plaques are a major histopathological hallmark of AD, the potential neuroprotective effects of CART against Aβ toxicity suggest that CART is a rational target in the search for therapies against this disorder. Furthermore, the mechanism underlying CART-mediated protection also warrants further investigation."

"In addition to modafinil showing potent effects on the sleep/wake system, it is clear that modafinil has noteworthy neuroprotective effects as well that involve some sort of antioxidative process. While these effects may be coincidental to modafinil's wake-promoting effects, the role of the ATP breakdown product adenosine in homeostatic sleep regulation is at least suggestive that modafinil's neuroprotective effects are not irrelevant to the consideration of modafinil's wake-promoting effects."

This is what I've found out, what I've learned. This is where it starts. It's like—I don't know—I've been thrown a salvation grenade, maybe. If it works, my foible—no, let's call it what it is, my weakness—might just save me from this nightmare.

It's enough.

It's hope.

The end